A Sensible Solution

Beth Poppet

To the late Alan Rickman, whose beautiful portrayal of Colonel Brandon necessitated a great deal more scenes between him and Marianne, and a faster resolution of marriage than Miss Austen provided. This entire novel owes its existence to the most endearing expression he made just after Marianne thanks him from bringing her mother to Cleveland.

Chapter One

Marianne sat up straight in bed, clutching the covers around her shaking form as she took great, heaving gasps of air. It had happened again; even in sleep her mind would not relent, and plagued her with the feelings and images of a day she would much rather leave forgotten in the past. She sank back into the covers, trying desperately to lie still and breathe quietly so as not to wake Elinor again.

She did not know—*could* not know the burden on her heart. For this was a pang too grievous to share; too ruinous for them all. It did not matter that *he* was in the wrong. The world did not forgive a ruined woman, regardless of who was to blame. There would be no justice for Marianne. There would be no happy marriage built on her foolish ideals of romantic love she once believed in. There would be no marriage at all were the scandal to be known. She shivered violently and not from the cold.

Being so incapable of showing feelings or expressing opinions which were not her own, neither was Marianne able to admit a change in sentiment, especially one so strong as her attachment to Mr. Willoughby of Allenham. She had once believed he still loved her, that his greatest sin was in loving her *too* much, and if she could only see him, speak to him, and assure him that she forgave any perceived trespasses he would not be ashamed to return to her and continue as they had been in Devonshire. She truly believed that his actions before his departure from Barton, though repugnant to all decency, were simply a consummation of his grand passion for her rather than a crime against her person, and she had come to town with the distinct purpose of proving her defence of him to be founded in truth. But the silence which her letters were met with was the first blow in a succession of hard realities to end her sad conviction, and the rest came in forms far harder to dismiss. Poor, foolish Marianne never would have thought the sullying of her innocence to be cruel until it was followed by a dismissal.

For weeks she had done little but pine and cling to the unfounded hope that the only thing keeping Willoughby from her was malicious slander that had reached his ear by way of some vile creature that wished her ill. Who might have cause to hate her so thoroughly, and succeed in turning his head so completely after all that had passed between them, even she could not easily conjure, but day by day as her sense of loss increased, Marianne found some new subject to imagine motive for the cruel act, and no amount of Elinor's caution would dissuade her from the suspicion.

However, several encounters with Willoughby,

and one appalling letter in his own hand drove the tender feelings and any hope of his acquittal out of Marianne's breaking heart. At the same time that she wrestled with the inevitable truth that Willoughby, and Willoughby alone was to blame for his actions, an awful suspicion regarding the consequence of those actions crept into her mind, and the stirrings of its beginning with the struggles of before created such a conflict of emotion that she was rendered quite unable to act as she was used to.

Marianne became pensive. She could hardly speak of her suspicions; neither could she enter into conversation with that open and impassioned nature of hers when she was so uncertain of her true feelings on anything that had ever mattered to her, now that Willoughby was a villain and it was possible she was to be cast down as the lowliest of wretches.

Becoming ill at the thought, Marianne fumbled with the cupboard at their bedside and retched into the *bourdaloue*. There was no escaping Elinor now. She would awaken and try to understand what troubled her sister.

Elinor was well aware all was not right with Marianne, but found her so distressed when pressed on the matter that she soon relented in her questioning and only asked how she could soothe the night terrors that had begun mere days ago. They had not crossed paths with Willoughby of late, and as no sister letter had arrived to distress Marianne anew, she could not conceive of anything that might shake her so.

Marianne could not offer reply to Elinor's

queries. Not only because she could not bear to tell of the whole sorry business, but the tenderness with which Elinor posed her questions brought such crippling sobs that it was impossible to speak a word. She could only cling to whatever was near enough to hold onto in the hopes that the feel of tangible objects would steady her in some small way.

She knew she must look horrific. Her eyes were sunken and glassy, her figure increasingly changing, to the point that even Mrs. Thornton commented on the ill fit of her gowns.

She would have liked to stay in and not show herself in society, whatever politeness demanded, but she could not avoid it. The Dashwood sisters had come to London expressly to enjoy its lively diversions, and to decline each invitation seemed a poor way to thank Mrs. Jennings for her hospitality. With each and every torturous obligation to go calling, to attend assemblies, and overall give the impression of a lady of enjoyment, Marianne found her only measure of comfort in the possibility of Edward's being present, for if her happiness was forever lost, she would not refuse an invitation that might further the happiness of her beloved sister.

But oh, it was hard! So very hard to have all of the worst confirmed by his outright slighting of her, witnessed by Marianne herself, in the interim of her most furious of struggles.

When first she had seen him since the dreadful affair, the pain had been acute, indeed. Though more than two months time had passed since he stood before her in the flesh, Marianne could not have fully prepared for the shock of suddenly spying him less than twenty steps away as they entered the crowded room. She was spared the torture of pretended niceties, as he was much engaged with the company of a fashionable young lady, who she would later learn the identity of. This too spared her the obligation of explaining her sudden inability to compose herself, and those close to her made up their own minds as to why her complexion turned deathly white, breath refused her lungs, and her legs buckled beneath her. Elinor and the Colonel had supported her feeble walk to the carriage but she could not so much as lift her head in gratitude for his help, though Elinor had the good mind to do so. Perceptive as she was, Elinor still thought her great distress was over the loss of Willoughby as a suitor; as if she pined for him and his attentions like the lovesick fool she had been. If only it were so. If only the unbearable ache in her heart and the twisting in her gut were from unrequited love, then she might more easily forget him as the Colonel surely had forgotten his infatuation with her.

But it was not unrequited. She knew in her heart, and if there were a deeper place to know such a thing, it was there too that Willoughby had loved her — *did* love her, and she could not so easily relinquish her long-stated belief that one did not love so completely only to forsake all in the face of fifty thousand pounds. It was not possible. It *should* not be possible.

As they did during such nights of anguish, Marianne found her thoughts turning to the Colonel and his behaviour in comparison to

Willoughby's. She had mocked his suit before; derided his age, and made sport of his sombre demeanour. How circumstances had changed! Now she was the one worthy of derision and mockery, and how he would count himself fortunate indeed for not openly attaching himself to a woman who would become so debased. Prudence did not seem so boorish and constricting to Marianne any longer. Elinor was right. She should have taken care. The mere thought of her past exhibitions were enough to make her stomach turn again.

The telltale sign of Elinor's consciousness was felt in the warm hand on Marianne's back. "Dearest, are you certain you are not ill?"

She dabbed the corner of her mouth with a towel and spoke with a steady voice. "I am quite well, Elinor. Or I shall be in the morning. It is only some bad poultry."

"We had the same supper, Marianne, and I did not lose mine in the chamber pot."

"You have always had a stronger constitution than I. Go back to bed. I assure you I am well," she lied.

With a small sigh that betrayed her scepticism, Elinor shifted back under the covers, struggling to find a new place of warmth after much of it had escaped the confines of the bed sheets.

Marianne knew she was selfish for not returning to her side at once and offering what added warmth she could to their coverlet, but tonight she felt the closeness oppressive and sleep only intensified the emotions she was loathe to dwell upon.

It might have been bearable, had he shown any sign of cruelty from the start. She then could have hated him better, berated herself for more specific failings of judgement. But he was perfect. So affable, attentive, and utterly charming. Even now it was difficult to think of the Willoughby who wooed her as the Willoughby who forced her to his bed on the day that should have brought about his proposal. Perhaps all men were such; hostile, manipulative braggarts who played a pretty part in order to have their way. But she could not believe that, truly. Though her trust had been permanently shaken, she could not believe such things of dear Edward. She could not believe them of Colonel Brandon.

Yet again, Marianne found herself wishing she were more like her sister. Wise, resolute Elinor, who never let her emotions get the best of her behaviour.

Marianne was resolute in one thing, and that was putting an end to a great portion of her troubles by confirming a nagging suspicion once and for all. Since she was unable to sleep, she readied everything she would require for her morning walk. The little yellow card with the pencilled address she took out from her bag and read once more, though she'd already memorised it with her continued staring. Her hair she plaited and pinned in a simple but serviceable style. The worn, black cloak that Elinor had wondered at her packing she kept hanging on the outside of the wardrobe so as not to make any additional noises by the opening of doors and cupboards when she decided to leave.

She had thought to go hours from now, nearer daybreak, but as the minutes passed and the silence in the room threatened to engulf her, she was overcome with a great anxiety to have done at once and not to wait for morning's first light.

She felt every bit of a woman of ill repute, slinking out of the apartment under the cloak of darkness, terrified that every flicker of light was intended to expose her and her destination. Where she was going was not too far. No one in Mrs. Jennings's company would ever travel to that part of the city on purpose, but it was as easy to find as it was to avoid. The only thing that mattered to her now was anonymity.

She prayed that Elinor would not wake too soon and rouse the house, fearing Marianne had run away in a fit of fancy. She was not prepared to flee Elinor's side and forge a life alone yet. Perhaps, if the question she was to have answered at the place of her destination yielded the discovery she feared, then she might consider the possibilities and manner of departure.

Tonight, however, she was simply tired and sore; sore of heart and sore of body. Her greatest fear lay not in what troubles awaited her down the dark alleyways of the hardened and desperate, but what discoveries might be brought to light by the end of her journey.

Chapter Two

Elinor awoke to the sound of Marianne's pen scratching hastily against the paper which she could only imagine to be an answer letter to Willoughby. Marianne was already dressed in a simple frock with almost no ornaments or ribbon of any kind; a strange thing for her sister. Not only a late dresser, Marianne was wont to dress as fine as possible even on the quietest of mornings, and Elinor thought it more than a little unusual that her drab, black cloak was hanging on the knob of the wardrobe as if recently utilised.

"Have you gone out?" she queried, still encumbered by a fog of sleep.

"Only for a walk," was her short reply.

"This early in the morning?"

The only sound she had in return was in the continued scratching of the pen.

"Dearest, I wish you would tell me..."

"Please, Elinor. Not now. I will tell you soon, but I need to be alone with my thoughts for the present. If I try to make sense of things before I'm ready..." The pen paused in its afflictions of the

9

paper for a second. "No. I will tell you soon, but you must not press me now."

"Very well," Elinor murmured. "Are you coming down to breakfast?"

"I must ask you to excuse me to Mrs. Jennings as I am not quite myself this morning."

"Shall I have something sent up for you?"

"Thank you, no. I could not eat for anything in this moment."

Breakfast was a quiet and somewhat gloomy affair, even with Mrs. Jennings present. Though she teased and wheedled her best with Elinor, she did not receive the same flushed features and ducked heads that Marianne or the Miss Steeles were wont to give, and she soon contented herself with remarking on the unlucky weather that kept all the sportsman out of doors and away from London society. Elinor would not venture to say she missed Mrs. Jennings's unchecked joviality, but no more did she welcome the shift in mood that permeated the entire household—or what was left of it now that the Steele sisters had gone to stay with Fanny for the remainder of their visit.

It was about the middle of the day, and Elinor was employed in writing a letter to her mother when Marianne entered the room, looking the face of death.

"Elinor..." she began haltingly, but seeing the letter set out and the ink drying fast on Elinor's pen she retracted. "Oh, you are busy. It can keep."

"No, stay! It is only a letter to Mama. You look positively ill, Marianne. Come and sit down. I'll have another cup of tea brought up." She moved to ring the bell, but Marianne stayed her hand.

"No, thank you. I could not drink it. I cannot..." Being overwhelmed with emotion, she brought a trembling hand to her forehead and sighed deeply. She was about to go on when a distinct knock startled her into a panic. "There is someone here!"

"It may have been for next door."

"That was not for next door! Good God, it is not Willoughby?" She appeared so agitated at the thought that Elinor was convinced she feared rather than desired his company.

Footsteps approached. Marianne stood from her chair and her eyes darted about as if to find some other escape that did not require her exit by the only door to and from the room. "I cannot face him today!" she exclaimed, and strode so hastily forward that she nearly collided with the Colonel as he stepped in. Her cheeks turned crimson and she wrung her hands in surprise.

"Colonel! Forgive me, I did not expect... You must excuse me, I am not well." And so saying, she fled to her chamber.

Elinor greeted him with more decorum and reserve. "Please forgive her, Colonel Brandon. She is not herself today."

Deep lines furrowed his brow and he seemed to be in a distress almost equal to Marianne's, though it was his way to show it in a far different manner. "Your sister is often out of spirits, it seems."

"I confess I am more than usually puzzled by her melancholy of late. I believe she confides in me as much as anyone, but I am at a loss as to how I might help her this time."

The expected pleasantries were exchanged; inquires as to the health of the youngest Miss

Dashwood and their mother, comments on the weather, and various nothings that must precede any discussion of worth. Elinor was aware that the Colonel was intent on bringing the conversation around to a specific topic, but not certain how to assist him, she paused in her answers to take a long sip of tea.

Finally, he took a quiet breath as if to rally himself and asked, "When am I to congratulate you on the acquisition of a new brother?"

"I'm not certain I understand you, Colonel."

"The engagement of your sister to Mr. John Willoughby is much talked of throughout town."

Elinor's expression betrayed sincere alarm. "This is surprising to me as Marianne has offered no such confidence to her family. If they are engaged, it should not be well known."

"Is it *quite* impossible, then — ?" here he abruptly stopped himself and seemed to reconsider. "Excuse me, Miss Dashwood. You must think me impertinent, but I came with the express purpose of inquiring whether or not things are firmly settled between your sister and Mr. Willoughby. Please tell me that of their poorly concealed relations, all that remains is their walk to the church, for only then will I deny myself the hope of ever succeeding with her."

The grave intensity with which he spoke went straight to Elinor's heart, as it indicated what profound feelings he had for Marianne. She could not think of how to answer him. Of the mutual affection Marianne and Willoughby shared, she was certain. Though the manner of their engagement was little known to her, and indeed, the lack of true correspondence seemed odd for two so desperately in love, Marianne's pining was clear and Elinor refused to give hope to the Colonel where there was none to be had.

"Though I cannot say with confidence that they are engaged, I have no doubt that she loves him and would have no hesitation in accepting his hand whenever it should be offered. I believe that... though we wait for the proper announcement, Marianne's affections are that of one already quite engaged."

He listened to her with silent attention, and on her ceasing to speak rose directly from his seat. After saying in a voice of emotion, "To your sister I wish all imaginable happiness; to Willoughby that he may endeavour to deserve her," he took his leave, and went away.

Elinor returned to the upper room with heavy heart. It was evident by his conduct and manner of speech that Colonel Brandon was quite in love with Marianne, and though she would not wish the matter settled for his sake, she feared any more waiting on Marianne's part might bring harm to her, whether by wasting away with little regard to her own health, or some romantic notion that might turn her head.

"What did the Colonel want?" Marianne asked with a listless sigh.

"Only to offer congratulations on your engagement to Willoughby."

She coloured and Elinor was surprised by the vehemence in her tone. "No, that cannot be true. You are teasing. Elinor. That isn't funny," she said severely. "Joking is not your strong suit; you should leave such devices to Margaret."

"I am quite serious. The news of Willoughby's preference for you in Devonshire has preceded his arrival here. Colonel Brandon says there is not much else talked of."

She paled then, and was thrown into a state of utter distraction. "Oh, Elinor...what am I to do? Oh, God! Whatever shall I do?"

Elinor took to her side, entreating her on her knees. "Dearest, you *must* tell me what troubles you! I cannot help you if you communicate nothing! Why does Willoughby not write to you? Why did he not acknowledge you at the assembly in favour of another woman? Have you quarrelled? What am I to make of all your unanswered letters and melancholy sighing? You are barely eating; you wander through rooms like a shadow; you are hardly the lively Marianne that I know and am both aggravated and endeared by. What is it, dear one?" Reaching a cool hand to her flushed cheek she pleaded, "Please, tell me. I have never seen you in such low spirits and it makes me anxious."

Marianne's head was turned towards the far corner of the chamber, but her eyes were unfocused as if she looked upon some tragic scene playing out before her and was not quite present in the room. The resignation in her voice terrified Elinor more than any previous outbursts of emotion.

"I am with child."

"Marianne..." Had Elinor not been kneeling she would have sought the nearest chair to catch herself in, for her body turned uncooperative to the task of standing.

"Confirmed only this morning while you slept,"

she breathed, never taking her focus from the corner of the room, "I slipped out to see an old woman who... Oh, Elinor..." her voice faded to a mere whisper and she looked her sister in the eye. *"What is to become of me?"*

It seemed a dreadful thing to ask, but Elinor was not willing to make anymore assumptions regarding her sister. "The child is Willoughby's?" she put carefully.

Marianne nodded piteously.

"You cannot wait for word from him any longer," Elinor insisted. "You *must* go to him in person and tell him to announce your engagement at once, the sooner to be married."

"We are not engaged," Marianne corrected her, "He has made me no promise. In that at least he is blameless, for he has broken no vow to me."

"No vow! Marianne, he took you to Combe Magna! He professed his love every day by each word, and look, and action. Though the words were never spoken, he behaved in a way that only men in love have warrant to, and now you carry his child! If he did not intend to marry you, he has used you most cruelly!"

"He has! He has used me! Oh, Elinor, yet I loved him!" With this she began to cry quite violently, and with such a pained look that Elinor was moved to her own tears of sympathy. "I loved him as he loved me!"

"But you are not engaged," she confirmed once and for all.

Marianne shook her head as she wept.

"Will you go to him then and ask he take responsibility?"

"No, Elinor. I will not. I cannot. There are things now I know of his character... do not ask me to speak of it, but I would not bind myself to such a man, even in such desperate straits as this. How am I to bear it?" she cried aloud, a great sob overtaking her. Soon, the emotion had quite exhausted her and she lay upon the bed continuing to bewail her miserable condition.

Elinor was at a loss for words. How could she comfort her poor sister when there was no comfort to be had? Marianne insisted that she would not go to Willoughby whatever the cause, and she must have her reasons. She wished she would tell them to her so that she might understand better or advise otherwise, but at present Marianne needed her sisterly presence and not her intrusive questioning.

The sudden entrance of Mrs. Jennings was not a welcome one. Worse still, was the news she brought; that Willoughby was now engaged to a Miss Grey with her fifty thousand pounds, and Mrs. Jennings was quite adamant about how shamefully he had used her dear friend in making everyone believe he was madly in love with her. Marianne's wails were begun anew, and Mrs. Jennings took her leave to find some treat with which to tempt her.

Elinor stayed by her side for the remainder of the day and took care of all the little comforts she was used to tending to whenever Marianne would let her. She behaved as if her every attention was on Marianne and the little tasks about the room, but all the while her thoughts were in a fog as she tried to imagine what was to be done or who they could possibly turn to for help.

Chapter Three

Elinor was most bewildered as to her sister's decision to continue to stay in London even though she was not intending to seek Willoughby out. More bewildering still was her refusal to take part in any discussion regarding a marriage to him. Yes, he was engaged; yes he was an abominable wretch for abandoning Marianne so, but in the eyes of society, unless she could be married and quickly, Marianne would soon have an irremovable blot on her character. For herself, Elinor was not so worried. She had already despaired of her own chances at happiness and it was for her sister alone she now strove and schemed. Despite anyone's feeling on the matter, the most sensible course seemed for Marianne to marry Willoughby.

Bringing it about might be difficult; impossible even with the financial strain the Dashwoods were under, but for Marianne to not even entertain the thought of trying... Elinor was hard pressed to understand it. She mused on the possibility of doing her best to bring it about without Marianne's approval. Perhaps if someone could pay

Willoughby a grand amount and everything was settled without her involvement, Marianne would see that there was no other way.

But who could possibly care to help them in such a fashion? Certainly not John. Even if her uncle was inclined to help in any way, the nature of their distress would only be cause for Fanny's scorn who would just as soon wash her hands of the whole business and persuade her husband to do the same. It was clear there would be no help from the Dashwoods.

She suspected that if Colonel Brandon was aware he would be moved to offer what assistance he could. There was no doubt he harboured great affection for Marianne and was a good and honourable man. He would not like her to suffer society's derision even under the circumstances of her degradation, though his willingness to assist did not matter as their situation was not something that might be brought to his attention through polite means.

Elinor was spared the torturous circles her mind was driving her to with the maid's sudden announcement of the Colonel himself.

This time, rather than beginning with dainty sips of tea and formal inquiries, they found it mutually beneficial to forgo all preliminary niceties. Elinor greeted him in earnest, thanking him for coming with no small emotion in her voice.

Colonel Brandon nodded once and tersely, telling her he needed no thanks for such an errand.

"How is your sister?" His tone was all concern and feeling, not willing to waste time on unnecessary stiffness.

"Marianne suffers cruelly," Elinor answered with a frankness that somewhat surprised even her. "I cannot... tell you the extent of all her troubles, for it is a burden not easily shared. However, I can say that circumstances being what they are, I am at quite a loss as to how I might help her. I tried to persuade her to come home, but she is resolved not to return to Barton for the duration of her... that is... forgive me, Colonel. It is impossible for me to continue without betraying her deepest confidence."

"Perhaps... I..." The Colonel lighted a finger on the back of the settee, skimming the curve of the back as he considered how he was to proceed. It was the most like losing his composure Elinor had ever witnessed in the Colonel, excepting the day he'd made haste to flee from their Delaford picnic. "Miss Dashwood, may I relate to you some circumstances which nothing but an earnest desire of being *useful*..."

Elinor's breath caught in her throat as she anticipated his intentions. "You have something to tell me of Mr. Willoughby." It was stated rather than put as a question. She had long sensed that the Colonel had more than one reason to dislike Mr. Willoughby, and he possessed too good a temperament for jealousy to rule his disdain absolutely.

Colonel Brandon inclined his head to confirm her suspicions and carried on. "When I had quitted Barton last — no. I must go further back. No doubt... *no* doubt," he emphasised, "Mrs. Jennings has apprised you of certain events in my past. The sad outcome of my connection to a woman called

Elizabeth."

Elinor assented that she had been informed of something regarding that history by Mrs. Jennings.

Haltingly — sometimes averting his gaze as if to recall a sorry detail from the past, or lowering his eyes to dwell on pleasanter thoughts — he continued. "Less commonly known is that twenty years ago, before she died, Eliza bore an illegitimate child. The father, whoever he was, abandoned them. Eliza begged me to look after the child. I had failed her in every other way; I could not refuse her now. I took the child, also Elizabeth — Beth, we called her — and she was raised with a family in the country. I admit... I spoiled her." This he spoke with a heavy sigh. "I allowed her too much freedom. Every indulgence I afforded her. Nothing was denied her that I could possibly offer, and I offered her much."

Here he paused as if reaching a particularly painful part of his narrative. "Almost a year ago, she disappeared. For eight months I was left to imagine the worst. On the day of the Delford picnic I had the news that would hasten me away to her. She was... with child, and the blackguard who had left her with no hint of his whereabouts..."

"Do you mean Willoughby?" Elinor finished hoarsely as she paled.

"It was his reprehensible dalliance with Beth that drove Mrs. Smith to cut him off unless he married her, and being steeped in debt and faced with the prospect of losing his only income, a marriage to your sister would have, in his mind no doubt, ruined him completely."

"So he abandoned Marianne for Miss Grey and

her fifty thousand pounds."

The Colonel seemed as pained to relate his account as Elinor was to hear it, but he said by way of defence, "I would not have burdened you had I not believed... in time, it might lessen your sister's regrets."

"Oh, Colonel, if you only knew the extremity of my sister's regrets..." unable to continue without spoiling Marianne's trust, she put a hand to her newly aching head and sighed.

"I have described Mr. Willoughby as the worst of libertines," the Colonel said, "but I have it on good authority that he did mean to propose that day, and would have were it not..." here he paused, meditated, and after a click or two from the little clock in the room he said, "Whatever his conduct may be, he did love your sister and would have married her had it not been..."

"For the money," she finished at last.

"I do wish," he said after an interval of strained silence, "that you might entreat your sister to return to her mother. I do not recommend that you thwart her outright; she must know her own mind and what situation will more positively affect her constitution. However, London gossip is never kind and I would hope her free of its retribution. If plans for travel are arranged I insist you permit me to accompany you and your sister on the journey to Barton. Furthermore, if I may be of any small service to you or to her, do not hesitate to send for me. I am utterly at your service."

"Thank you, Colonel," Elinor said with feeling, "We are so thankful for your kindness. I know I may speak for Marianne in this regard, though she may not have the strength of mind to say so at present."

As was his custom, he nodded his understanding, only this time it was accompanied by the faintest of smiles.

After the Colonel had departed, Elinor took a tray up to Marianne. She was still stricken with melancholy but she made an effort to try a little of everything Elinor had brought in order to please her, and the teapot was a great deal lighter when it was taken down than when it had gone up.

When Elinor was satisfied that she had eaten all she was able, she told Marianne the entirety of the conversation that had passed between herself and the Colonel. Marianne listened with no interruption, choosing rather to gaze listlessly at the floor, but there was no doubt to Elinor that she gave her full attention.

At the last, Elinor remarked, "At least you may be certain that he loved you."

"Perhaps in his way," Marianne murmured forlornly and dabbing at a crumb on her gown, "But not as he should have."

Elinor had no sentiments of encouragement to relay so she turned to matters more practical.

"As for the Colonel... Marianne, I believe he may be our only hope for aid."

Marianne coloured at his mention and her features became altogether more alert. "How can you possibly imagine the Colonel is in a position to help us?"

"He is all kindness and concern, and I do not think he will turn you away if you ask him. Look at how he helped those poor girls before."

"But to grovel for aid... No, Elinor," she said at her sister's pained expression, "You must not think me too proud. It is not the act of seeking help that is so repugnant, but the fact that I must tarnish the image that good man has of me. I am so ashamed. Worse, I am the lowest of the low! How can I face him?" New tears began to trail down her cheeks, and Elinor felt her own heart breaking for her.

"What else are we to do? I will go to him myself if you prefer, dearest. But we have no connections, no money with which to force Willoughby to marry you. I cannot contrive of anyone else that might have the means and willingness to help us unfortunate sisters."

"Surely you are not suggesting that I ask the Colonel for help in persuading Willoughby to marry me!" Marianne cried. "I will not listen to such a notion! Even were he to be dissuaded from the great fortune of Miss Grey, which would require an enormous sum, to be trapped in a marriage with such a... a false man, always wondering if one bad turn or misfortune will send him galloping off to find money by any means; to live with a faithless scoundrel who may abandon us the moment hardships arise or he no longer finds me an amusing diversion to his gambling? No, you cannot be so unjust as to suggest it, Elinor."

"Perhaps you need not marry Willoughby, but what else are we to do? Where are you to go? I only mean that whatever your path might be, there is no more sensible solution than to seek the Colonel's help."

For a little while, Marianne mused in silence,

taking in all her sister had told her.

"Is it sensible?" she murmured after a time, more to herself than for Elinor's benefit.

What did she know of being sensible after all? If Elinor said it was so, she would believe it to be true; absurd as it sounded that the austere and upright Colonel Brandon would want anything to do with such a wretched woman as herself. But she had promised to take her sister's counsel from now on, and if Elinor said that seeking the Colonel's help was sensible and right she would do it, however ridiculous it seemed to her own mind.

And what a respite it would be to be put up somewhere secretly so as not to wound her mother, disgrace her sisters, and be exposed to the cruel consequences of a ruined reputation. The hope that such thoughts awakened in her made her restless to begin seeking help at once.

As she brushed the crumbs from off her covers with a heart somewhat lightened by having a plan of action to take on the morrow, she realised that for the first time in a very long while, Elinor's sense and her own sentiments were in perfect agreement.

Chapter Four

Colonel Brandon's London flat was situated on a quiet cobblestone street, away from the centres of gossip and marketplace activity; virtually everything Mrs. Jennings and her party had expressly come for. Not Marianne. She had come for her sister, to do everything in her power to promote Elinor's happiness since her own was so entirely ruined. Perhaps even now she came to Colonel Brandon for the sake of the same. Had her error marked only herself for desolation she might have returned to her mother to languish away, but she could not be a blight on Elinor's chance at a respectable and loving union with Edward. If there was any hope of such a union now, she knew she had best find a way to remove herself from the society of those she loved best in all the world; her mother and sisters.

Such were her thoughts as she and Elinor were ushered in. Such was her determination as they stood before the doorway that would lead to Colonel Brandon. She could bear any humiliation, any reproach, any look or word of revulsion, so long as by the end of it there was still hope for her sister.

"I should like to speak with him alone, dear Elinor."

"Are you certain?"

"Yes, quite certain."

"Very well. I will wait just outside for you if you've need of me."

"Dear, sweet Elinor," she said a little wistfully, letting her gloved hand linger a moment within the safe keeping of her sister's grasp before letting the servant show her in.

Colonel Brandon was expecting them, yet he gave a slight start as she entered, almost as if he was uncertain of how to receive her. He inclined his head in the same gentlemanly and formal way he had always done, yet there was something distracted—nervous, even, in his demeanour as he bid her sit. Despite the distressing nature of their interview, Marianne was not blind to the richness of her surroundings. The magnitude of his wealth must be great indeed if this was the state of his rarely used apartment.

She was surprised by how steady her voice was at the start. "Thank you, Colonel, for your prompt reply to my sister's letter."

Here, he stopped her with a brusque wave of his hand. "No. No thanks, please, I beg you. Your coming here today is just as I would have wished. I am thankful Miss Dashwood asked my counsel, for I was anxious to be of service even before I knew you might desire it."

This was a surprising revelation to Marianne, though not at all an unwelcome one. His assurances were puzzling, yet they bolstered her confidence in speaking more openly to him. "Elinor has told me of your kindness in regards to the woman who was... sorely used by Mr. Willoughby. I know I have no right to ask it of you; you are under no obligation whatever..." here her voice threatened to break and she struggled to go on as before, "But I find myself in a similar situation and I am forced to plead for your help. I do not ask for money!" she added with haste, "Only some advice on where I should go. How I might hide away for a time until I may perhaps return to my mother without anyone knowing... Perhaps I could work in a milliner's shop, or find some respectable employ under the guise of being a widow. I am not too proud. I only seek to keep this stain from polluting my family's good name and destroying my sisters' prospects."

"Miss Marianne," the Colonel replied, a deep frown setting his features quite grim, "Your sister was unable to relate your situation in full due to the delicate nature of certain subjects. So although I may have my suspicions, I am not fully aware..." He closed his eyes briefly and then opened them again. "That is to say... Are you with child?"

She nodded piteously. "Confirmed only two days ago." The tears began to trickle down her cheeks and she was too tired even to reach her handkerchief to her eyes. The weariness was beyond anything she had ever felt. It was akin to hopelessness, and she frightened herself with the emptiness it wrought.

He moved several paces behind his desk, eventually stopping with his back turned to her. He breathed a heavy sigh before turning round again.

"I know of no place where you might go without being recognised, unless it is far away in some hidden corner of the countryside. You could not work in your condition, nor would I have you do so. If I am to help you... and I mean to, certainly, I will not have you risk your own health by putting you in a workhouse. Nor will I further damage your reputation by placing you somewhere you might be discovered. However..." He chose his words carefully; guarded and precise even with such a distasteful subject to be discussed, "Though the utmost care would be used in discretion, if it is found out that it was by my efforts you were secured a living, your sisters might still be ruined as society does not look kindly on... kept women."

"Oh," she stopped him short with an exclamation, "I could not have you give me a home and a living! Not only for the hurt it would cause my family, but for your sake as well! I do not expect, nor even ask for anything more than counsel. Of course, I will never speak of this conversation to another living soul! You must not imagine me such a base creature as that."

Though he was frowning still, she did not think it a look of repulsion or anger. "If you will not accept a living from me, I see only one solution. We must marry at once, before your condition begins to reveal itself."

The silence that followed was not only long, but palpable.

"Colonel Brandon, I did not think you a jesting man."

"I assure you I speak in the greatest sincerity."

At this, Marianne lost all control of her emotions. Though she struggled to maintain her composure, the confusion was too great, the offer too incredible, and the onslaught of tears was overwhelming.

"Please, do not distress yourself, Miss Marianne. I am well aware that this marriage is not by any means what you would have desired for yourself, but rest assured that under my protection and care you will want for nothing, in comfort at least."

She hadn't the fortitude to explain her outburst. She was not distressed over the prospect of being the Colonel's wife, but the unthinkable kindness that he now extended to her. He did not even know the circumstances of her degradation but was willing still to attach her to his name, title, and fortunes in order to save her family from scandal. It was beyond all reason; beyond any contrivance of aid she could have hoped for.

"Colonel, I promise it is not from apprehension of being attached to you in such a permanent way that causes my distress. But you cannot know how thankful I am. The debt I owe you is one of such profound... I do not understand it! Indeed, I do not deserve it!"

"There are many things in this world we are not deserving of, Miss Marianne. If we all received our just desserts, I venture to say not a fellow alive would be happy."

"I will not be a nuisance! I will be the quietest, most unobtrusive wife to you."

"I ask for no such conditions. Please, do not burden yourself with worry. I only ask that you take your rest in the expanse of Delaford. It will allow you to be near your family without the exposure of scandal."

"How can I ever...?"

"Please." The Colonel seemed greatly troubled by her expressions of thanks and put her off from them as best he was able. "I will hear no more on debt or gratitude. I am not... a young man, Miss Marianne, and I find my disposition is not suitable to the romantic pursuits necessary for the wooing of ladies." At this, Marianne turned crimson, knowing how ardently she would have supported such a view mere weeks ago. "I do, however, still desire to establish a family for myself, and though you may not at first think of me in the way of a husband, I confess there is no other lady I would rather grace my estate. You cannot be... entirely unaware of my fondness for you, and I find it difficult to conceive of a man contemptible enough to abandon his..." He faltered, overcome by some emotion Marianne could not perceive. "But he has done it before, and I will have no more of your proffered thanks. I am not without gain in this situation, and you must forgive the selfish motives which urge me to this conclusion."

"Colonel Brandon, I cannot allow that there is any need for forgiveness. Whatever your gain in our union, it can be precious little in comparison to the immense burden you are undertaking!"

The slight widening of his smile evidenced his amusement. "Do you seek to dissuade me from this venture by your self-disparaging? Or am I meant to confess the boorish quality of my nature along with other deficiencies in exchange for trifling ones of your own? Let us not quarrel over which of us is the worse qualified to enter into matrimony, Miss Marianne. My vast years of experience give me an unfair advantage to the debate."

Marianne's eyes furrowed suspiciously. "You are teasing me, I think. I have never been able to respond to clever people with the proper tact called for, so you must forgive me if I defer. Elinor is much more suited to an exchange of wits during a crisis."

"Are you cross with me, Miss Marianne?"

The lady's blush deepened and she dipped her head in apology. "I am sorry. I promised not to be troublesome, and already I am provoking a quarrel."

"And I have already told you it was an unnecessary promise; one I will not hold you to." He turned the subject as her expression continued to convey her mortification. "Still, I think we should conclude the matter here. Your sister awaits you, does she not?"

"Yes, poor Elinor! I had almost forgotten her!"

This only furthered her distress, much to the Colonel's chagrin who hastened to lead her outside, but Marianne stopped him before the door. "If you will not accept my gratitude in words, at least accept this," she requested as she extended her hand most elegantly. "I know we are not gentlemen striking a business arrangement, but it would give me some peace of mind to join hands in an amiable manner."

He took it then, blinking and hesitant at first, but softening as his large, roughened hand encompassed hers entirely. He applied to it the faintest of pressure, and something very like a smile moved at the corner of his mouth. Seeming to come to himself he suddenly released it and said, "We should not keep Miss Dashwood waiting."

Though Marianne had done her utmost to maintain a level of composure since the beginning of their interview, her emotions were thoroughly wrung by the end of the matter, and seeing the thinly veiled anxiety of Elinor's features while considering the life she had narrowly escaped made the method of her rescue all the more poignant.

"Oh, Elinor!" she cried, and bursting into tears anew, flung herself into her arms, weeping into her shoulder.

"Whatever is the matter?" Elinor looked to the Colonel for an answer, utterly confounded.

Stoic as ever, he did not answer her directly but rather gave orders as one still commanding his officers. "Miss Dashwood, would you be so good as to stand witness? I intend to ask Sir John to accompany us with all haste and secrecy."

"I will do whatever you ask if it will help Marianne, but I cannot understand you. You wish me to stand witness for what occasion?"

"Our wedding," he answered gruffly. "I have asked, and Miss Marianne has agreed to marry me."

Chapter Five

The journey to Dorsetshire was difficult for Marianne. Though the weather was most obliging for travel—being neither too warm for the horses, nor damp for the roads—and though she knew the wearisome miles would bring her to a place of promised solace and security, each jolt and jerk of the coach was especially trying for her. She had gone weeks without proper sleep, and now that the worst of her fears of ruination and wretchedness was behind her, she wanted nothing more than to have a still, quiet place to reacquaint herself with the repose only a good night's sleep could afford. She was not naturally disposed to a strong constitution, but the affliction of a heavy heart was a burden that made any physical ailment increase her suffering tenfold. Now that her heart was eased of one of its greatest burdens, she was not oppressed with the sleeplessness that the anxieties of an uncertain future produced, nor was she prone to impassioned weeping upon every new hour. Still, the affects of suffering both in weeks of succession had taken their toll, and she was weary to the core.

Elinor sat beside Colonel Brandon upon their uniform insistence that Marianne be given the entire seat across to herself. Colonel Brandon bid the driver make frequent stops wherever it was convenient to do so without delaying their arrival by too much, and had provided Marianne with such a number of pillows that were she not at odds with her breakfast she would have been more than comfortable. As it was, she longed for them to reach their destination, and perhaps for Elinor to be a little less attentive, for it made her ill to have to speak to her in return.

Elinor had her own reasons for so frequently asking after her sister's comfort. She could tell that Marianne was unwell and had been unwell since they'd set off, but Marianne seemed determined to pretend otherwise. Though Elinor had caught her several times passing a hand over her stomach with a grimace, or wearily leaning against a pillar so that her head pressed against the cold stone, any attempt to address these signs of distress were met with deceptively cheerful rebuttals and absolute denial, the latter becoming especially forceful in the presence of Colonel Brandon.

Elinor doubted that her sister understood the extent of the Colonel's affection for her. To Marianne, love was all fire and passionately expressed platitudes of undying devotion. To her, love would not forebear silence — it could not endure patience, and Colonel Brandon's ardour was the epitome of such virtues that eluded her so miserably. The wrong done to her by Willoughby had tempered her view on matters of the heart, and cooled some of that feverish perspective, but not so much as to grant her by instantaneous revelation how deeply Colonel Brandon could feel, and certainly did feel for her.

She knew that Marianne wondered at his goodness in marrying her. She knew that it was an inestimable sense of gratitude that now guided her behaviour towards him, though a mutual affection was yet wanting. Marianne understood, and even spoke aloud to Elinor of what an expense the Colonel must have undergone to secure the special license for their marriage, of the sacrifice he was making in so hastily securing her a home and husband with no conceivable gain to his own person. She cheerfully donned her best gown with Elinor's assistance, and followed with minute detail every line of the Colonel's instructions concerning place and appointment for their union with an applied determination Elinor had scarcely seen in her before. It was not urged by a fondness for the good Colonel who took her as wife, however, but a fear that if the union was delayed for any reason, there was a risk he might refuse to take part in the proceedings after all. At this, Elinor could only shake her head in secret grievance for the sake of her brother-in-law, whose tender expression towards Marianne during their exchange of vows, and small but insistent smile when their union was confirmed by the final pronouncement of the bishop made his personal benefit in the match all too clear.

Despite her inability to comprehend the depth of Colonel Brandon's emotions, there was a change in Marianne, and it was made evident by how carefully she tried to dismiss the symptoms of her condition, so aware was she of the difficulties he put upon himself in taking her to wife.

Marianne, who never failed to express the smallest of grievances, be they fact or fancy; Marianne, who took great pains to ensure that her own misfortunes were felt deeply by all those around her, no matter the injury to social decorum or inconvenience to others, now seemed determined not to let either a word or expression pass that might betray any of her complaints to her new husband.

Elinor was not sorry for this change, but neither was she used to it, and although she feared she pestered Marianne with her frequency of questioning, her sister gave no indication of being annoyed by the constant attention, and so it continued.

It was near nightfall when the coach pulled up to the drive, and Marianne was startled awake by the sudden ceasing of the clomping hooves and motion of the carriage as she had managed to doze for some fitful hours during the final stretch of their journey. Her short slumber made her no less eager to be shown to her room, and she was exceedingly grateful to the Colonel for making haste in helping her to alight from the coach.

A line of servants was there to greet them before the doors, and Marianne made a great effort to appear engaged during her introduction as the new mistress of Delaford—an effort which exhausted her thoroughly. No sooner had they crossed the threshold than her guise gave way and her fatigue made her sway on her feet. She would have stumbled into a heap on the foyer if it wasn't for her husband's ready arm to catch and steady her.

She had recovered her balance almost at once, and apologised for her clumsiness with an unaffected sincerity that Elinor thought suited this new Marianne very well.

Colonel Brandon dismissed her apology as one might dismiss a rambunctious puppy that collides with a stationary leg as he expertly gave directions to several servants to busy themselves with different tasks, including one to show Miss Dashwood to her room.

Elinor was about to protest that she should see to Marianne before retiring, but with a sudden realisation that Marianne was not her responsibility any longer, nor need she fear that the utmost might not be done for her with Colonel Brandon as her champion, she had nothing more to do but follow the servant up to her room. She would leave for Barton Cottage just as soon as she was certain Marianne had no more need of her. Secretly, she hoped Marianne might ask her to stay a while yet, so that she might see her settled and comfortable as mistress here, but if the invitation was not given directly, Elinor would not seek one out.

Marianne was so tired that she hardly acknowledged her whereabouts until the Colonel had helped her to a chaise lounge in a grand and elegant bedroom. She thought it almost too fine for a lady's chamber and was about to say so, when catching her blunder she asked instead, "Are these your rooms? They are very fine."

The Colonel offered her one of his slight smiles at her approval. "I thought it prudent for the present to at least appear to be sharing a chamber. Your rooms will be fitted out to your liking on the morrow, but for tonight..." Here he left the thought unfinished. "My staff is loyal and not prone to gossip, yet I would leave no room for suspicion when the time comes for your condition to be made known."

"Ah, that is... very... I had not thought..." she sighed at her own inability to think of anything beyond how dearly she wished to sleep. She had not even considered the possibility of Colonel Brandon insisting upon his husbandly rights. They had begun their travels directly following their marriage, and he had behaved no differently to her than he always had, albeit with less hesitance in the arm outstretched, or a steadier gaze than a mere acquaintance might be warranted to. The fact that such a significant part of the marriage covenant had not occurred to her as something that might pass between her and the Colonel both unsettled and frustrated her. Colonel Brandon was not so very old as to repel all notion of intimacy, but neither was she prepared to share such intimacies so soon after the way in which Willoughby had used her. Still, she could not be so ungracious as to deny him outright if he insisted upon their sharing a marriage bed.

"You should sleep," he said with some concern over her darkened features, instantly putting to rest any likelihood of acting upon her anxieties. "I will send Hannah in to help you prepare for bed."

His hand was on the door when Marianne stayed him with a question that surprised them both.

"You will return?" Husbandly rights or no, she did not relish the thought of his being forced to sleep in less than acceptable quarters in order to accommodate her presence.

"Do not worry on my account. I am often away, and when I am not, I usually retire in the bedroom adjoining. It is on rare occasion that I take advantage of these quarters. You will not be depriving me of expected comforts."

"Then let this be one of those occasions," she proffered. "I am used to sharing a bed. With my sisters," she was hasty to amend. "And if we are to give the servants the proper impression that we are... fully married..." she was not willing to say more, exhaustion and politeness withholding further detail.

"Very well," he relented. "I will come by the adjoining chamber once you are made comfortable."

Marianne had long learned to do without the help of servants, but tired as she was she found it most agreeable for the buttons and hooks and laces of her attire to be undone by another.

Hannah was a tidy, middle-aged woman who had no scruples against seeing to her charge in complete silence, and by the time she had Marianne properly outfitted in her nightclothes and plait, and quit the room, Marianne was in such a state of drowsiness that if the Colonel did return to their shared chamber, she was entirely unaware of when he entered or when he rose again to depart.

The late hour in which she awoke, and the rumpled state of disarray that the sheets had been reduced to, made her blush to think of the impression such a sight would give. It was strange indeed to so unwittingly be aiding the deception that would be her saving, and she became determined to add what other details she might in order to leave no doubt in the minds of the servants that the Colonel and she were lawfully and entirely married.

It struck her then that she had bled that first encounter with Wiloughby, and she feared the absence of blood on the sheets might put her reputation as well as Colonel Brandon's at risk. She swept her gaze about the room for some object she might use to cut herself, but the room was furnished solely for sleeping and marital congress; there was no cabinet or desk that promised any implement by which her devices might be realised.

Finally, she spied the sharp edge of a gilded frame which was hanging low enough on the wall to produce the desired blood after she'd struck her arm deliberately against the corner. She staunched the wound with the sheets, most satisfied with her quick thinking, until she realised she had nothing with which to bind or cover her injury.

If she could but find her way to her own chamber, perhaps the hem of an old petticoat would do the trick and she could bind her arm and dress quickly before the maid could recognise the deception. However, she did not know which door led to her room. So fatigued was she the night before that she hardly remembered which door she and the Colonel had entered by, and she could not risk coming upon a servant in the wrong chamber while stripped to her shift and holding a bleeding arm.

It was in this delicate moment of Marianne's indecision that one of the three bedroom doors was opened and the housekeeper came in with the tea tray.

Chapter Six

The intolerable lapse of silence which pervaded the room was broken at last by the careful questioning of the housekeeper, after she had set the tea tray down on the service table.

"Madame, are you hurt?"

Marianne tightened her grip around the self-inflicted injury as her eyes searched wildly for some means of escape, but found none by way of either falsehood or flight. She conjured half a dozen ridiculous lies in a moment, but before any of them could pass her lips, the housekeeper had taken in the sight of the tangled, blood-stained sheets, and seemed to comprehend what Marianne was about.

Rather than step back in scandalised horror, or seem amused by the sight, her eyes flickered with kindly concern and she took a bold step forward. "Oh, mistress, forgive me, but may I speak plainly?"

"I would much rather you do so than leave me to wonder what you must think of me," she replied with some annoyance.

"You mustn't worry that you didn't bleed," she

said, head dipped slightly and voice lowered to convey a quiet conference. "It doesn't always happen, you know. And if it doesn't, it means you've a good, and gentle man who takes care of you properly, do you see?"

Marianne did not see, exactly, but she was willing to be enlightened, however humiliating the situation of being taught the ways of marital intimacy by a housekeeper on her first day as mistress.

"Having three daughters grown and married, and a husband of my own, I can tell you this; if you bleed from—I beg your pardon—from intercourse, whether it's the first time or the hundredth time, it means *he's* done something wrong, and not the other way 'round. The Colonel is a man of the world. I assure you he won't question your innocence by a lack of blood on the sheets, and neither will I."

Marianne was at a loss for a proper reply, and so she continued to stare blankly while the servant continued.

"Perhaps in another household, you might have cause for worry about the servants' talk, but here, with all so loyal to the Colonel and with me to keep them in line you have nothing to fear."

Marianne shivered a little, overcome by the kindness of the woman before her, and relief that she had not fallen under suspicion.

"Has Hannah not brought you your morning gown?" the housekeeper wondered indignantly, mistaking Marianne's shiver for one of physical discomfort. "Never mind that, yet. Let's get rid of these sheets and find you a dressing gown, first.

You can take your tea and I'll send someone to patch your arm when I'm done with the bedding. I'll take it myself, so you can be sure there'll be no trouble with the maids."

Remembering the unlikely lady's maid who had dressed her for bed the night before, and the peculiarity of her age and station, Marianne asked, "Has Hannah been long with the family?"

"Yes, ma'am. Almost all her life. Longer than I have, that's for certain." The familiar trickle of water being poured over tea leaves and the pleasant clink of the spoon against cup as Marianne directed her preferences of sweetness were welcome sounds. "I know she's too old to be a proper lady's maid; her days of beauty have long passed, and she doesn't know the new styles to keep up with the fashionable ladies of the ton. It must seem very odd to you that the Colonel would keep her in his employ." Here she paused to hand Marianne her tea and let her savour a taste to ensure it was to her liking. "She was trained at quite a young age to be lady's maid to the Colonel's mother, you see, and when Mrs. Brandon passed on, the old housekeeper intended to send her elsewhere. For one reason or another, they never found her a suitable new position and so she stayed on, more or less as an upper housemaid. I might have dismissed her, being that it seemed so unlikely that the Colonel would marry, and if he did it was expected his wife would bring her own lady's maid—no offence intended, Madame, I only meant to say that since he never imagined any lady could enter his heart since the end of his first tragic love... well, he's allowed me to keep her on all these years out of kindness to her, I know."

The housekeeper finished tucking the sheets into a neat bundle so that none of the blood stain was visible, and stood holding it against her as if it was merely folded linens, and part of her ordinary business to dispatch of bloodied sheets.

"Now, I hope I haven't said too much," she added. "If she displeases you, I'll begin searching for her replacement at once."

"No, I thank you," Marianne replied. "That will not be necessary. It is just as well she knows nothing of the new styles since my days of high fashion are at an end. I must dress simply and prudently, now."

The housekeeper looked as if she wished to say a great deal in reply to such a surprising declaration from her young and pretty mistress, but thought better of it.

"Forgive me," Marianne said, "I have forgotten your name."

"Mrs. Pickard, if it please you, mistress."

Marianne offered a small smile. "Mrs. Pickard, you have done me a great service today and I am most grateful."

Mrs. Pickard nodded, her dark eyes crinkling slightly at the edges with her warm smile, and Marianne had to struggle with the absurd thought that this woman might be closer in age to the Colonel than she was. Not for the first time that morning, she was embarrassed to be so young and in such a position.

"Now, if you'll forgive me, Madame, I've nothing to dress your wound with here, but I'll be just a moment and back again soon with some bindings for your arm."

Marianne sat contemplating all she'd been told and imbibed on one of Mrs. Pickard's sweet biscuits as she struggled to ignore how her arm was beginning to throb. She felt utterly foolish. When she had been but a girl and made an innocent, yet laughable remark about the producing of offspring, Elinor had taken it upon herself to grant her certain factual explanations of what occurred between a husband and wife. Marianne, however, had quickly dismissed her as an authority on the subject in favour of romantic novels and poetry. Once again, she berated herself for not listening to Elinor more seriously.

When the door was opened to admit Mrs. Pickard, it was to Marianne's abject horror that she saw she was not alone, for though the efficient housekeeper came laden with a basket of bandages and ointment for the wound, her own figure was dwarfed by the presence of Colonel Brandon who followed just behind.

He relieved the housekeeper of her supplies and dismissed her, assuring the woman that he would tend to her mistress himself. Once the housekeeper departed, leaving them alone, Colonel Brandon astonished Marianne by the prompt removal of his coat which he tossed nonchalantly over the bed. She watched in confusion as he then unbuttoned his cuffs and rolled up his sleeves until they stopped just short of his elbows. He then proceeded to wet the cloth with water from the wash basin and took up the seat beside Marianne.

"Let me see your arm," he insisted.

Mortified, Marianne put her empty teacup aside

and did as she was instructed; glad that he remained intent on the task of tending to her, and did not seem to notice the crimson blush that had bloomed across her cheeks. She was keenly aware of the lack of proper dress upon both their persons, and although she understood the necessity in his removal of coat and undoing of cuffs, she was grateful he did not make much of it, but examined her arm with singular attention.

Colonel Brandon's age in that moment conveyed neither infirmity nor handicap to his young wife. Indeed, in his steady application of the wet cloth, his gentle cleansing of the wound, and deft and careful binding of it, Colonel Brandon looked no more physically inadequate than mentally unsound. Marianne could not have boasted the same, considering appearances at present, and she took this new revelation to heart.

She caught herself watching his handiwork with rapt fascination. His hands were a great deal larger than Willoughby's, and one might have considered them unsuited for such delicate work if they had not borne witness to the results. Certainly, they were not as smooth and elegant as Willoughby's hands either, but there was a reverent patience in the manner of their use that had been sorely wanting in the younger man. Such comparisons allowed undesirable memories to pervade her mind, and Marianne shut her eyes against them, searching for some way to sufficiently distract her wandering thoughts.

With the slight pressure of Colonel Brandon's fingers closed around her forearm, she chose to dwell on his ministrations, and wonder what manner of tidings Mrs. Pickard had brought him to prompt his coming to her so quickly.

She found herself speaking aloud in an effort to divert her thoughts. "You said your servants are loyal, but I did not expect them to exhibit quite so much haste in reporting each trifling blunder of mine," she said, petulance lacing her tone.

"I would hardly consider this 'trifling,'" was his grave rebuttal, and he traced his thumb just above the freshly cleansed wound to better emphasise his point. "Are you cross with Mrs. Pickard for informing me of your injury? She knows I am better suited than the servants for patching up hurts. I believe your chances for a full recovery are good," he remarked with a playful smile, "but if you would rather I send for a doctor, I will do so."

"No!" she cried emphatically; then composing herself a little, "I thank you, no. It was not the injury I alluded to, but the conversation that transpired between us. I... did not know... I did not mean to give a bad impression of you." Her blush deepened at the admission. "I had thought... Because of him, I assumed it would always be so."

"I'm afraid I don't understand you," his hands faltered but only slightly as he wound the clean strips of cloth around her arm. "Mrs. Pickard told me nothing of your conversation, only that you were hurt. Of what are you speaking?"

Marianne supposed that if he had no scruples against partially undressing before her, there was no reason to withhold her full meaning. Her lip quivered and her heart quickened as she said in a quiet voice, "I did this on purpose in order to stain the bed sheets. I thought I would fall under suspicion otherwise, and besmirch your good name in the process. I did not know... I thought there should be proof of my innocence, however falsified."

"Mis..." he stumbled at her old title, "Mrs. Brandon, can it... be possible...?"

Marianne started at the use of her new name — her proper name as it now was — and inexplicably trembled at the way he released his hold of her arm, only to claim her hand instead and meet her gaze beseechingly.

"I *must* ask you something most serious, and I hope you will honour me with the absolute truth, for it is my duty as your husband and guardian to know. Were you..." He closed his eyes but for a moment, and Marianne was nearly overcome with the urge to reach out and comfort him, so pained was his expression. "Were you a willing participant in the manner of your child's conception?"

Marianne's breath caught in her throat and her trembling grew even more severe. In her wildest imaginings, she had never supposed it would be put to question whether or not she was willingly seduced, and most certainly not by the Colonel. It had not even occurred to Elinor to ask, so confident was she and all their acquaintances, that Marianne was so thoroughly infatuated with Willoughby there was nothing he could suggest that might be rejected by her.

Colonel Brandon was deeply moved by Marianne's struggle to speak, but said nothing further to urge her on, rather waiting with perfect forbearance while she spoke in great, heaving gasps that grew more like sobs with each successive word. The weight of his question still hung in the air. *Were you willing...?*

"I was not!" she shook with the emotion of being able to say the words aloud, equal parts relief and anguish. "I did not... encourage it! I did not *want* him to..." here she was disturbed by another series of heavy gasps as she expelled the next words. "I tried to resist! At the start, I swear I did! But I was so frightened of him leaving me if I continued to refuse that I did not struggle in the end. But he *has* left me! And he did not love me after all!" The violence of her emotions made her weak again, and she was soon pressed into the Colonel's side while she expended herself with her grief.

If Colonel Brandon was not so practiced in self-possession, he might have left Marianne in her distress, the sooner to find Willoughby and strangle him with his own two hands. As it was, he steadied himself for the sake of the unhappy creature that found some measure of comfort in leaning upon his shoulder, and perhaps by heaven's great gift, even needed him here with her. In an instant of reckless abandon, he ventured to draw her a little closer, and bring his other arm around to enfold her in a true embrace.

When the worst of her crying was ended, Marianne was struck with a sudden fear that caused her to pull away from his hold in order that she might plead with him anew. "You will not speak of this to Elinor, will you?! Poor Elinor! How it would break her heart to know the truth!"

His frown deepened, though she did not understand the reason. "Mrs. Brandon, you cannot suppose *me* to be immune to heartache, can you?"

"No, Colonel. I am sorry," she said, dabbing her eyes with the handkerchief he pressed into her hand. "What have I said wrong? Are you displeased with me?"

"Far from it, I assure you," he said gruffly, doing his utmost to hide the great anguish of heart he silently suffered. "Now if you feel able to walk a few paces with my assistance, I will take you to your own room where you must eat what I send up to you, and rest for the remainder of the afternoon. There is an urgent matter I must see to."

"Will you send Elinor to me?" she asked, brightening at the thought of her sister's company. "You will not let her leave for Barton yet, will you?"

Colonel Brandon smiled affectionately into the tear-stained eyes of his wife. "Your sister may stay as long as she wishes. If it would please you both, let her call Delaford home too for as long as she remains unmarried."

At these words, Marianne felt a fresh wave of emotion threaten to overpower her, and she grasped his offered arm with both her hands, the better to draw strength from, and be led to her rooms with the help of her husband.

Chapter Seven

The door closed softly behind Colonel Brandon, and he permitted himself a length of time to simply stand by her chamber and expel his ire by regulated breathing, thereby allowing some of his hotter emotions to dissipate before he ventured to conduct business in a rational manner.

That Willoughby was a scoundrel of the blackest kind, he was already well aware. That Willoughby found diversion in seducing young women and fleeing the consequences of his sinful pursuits, he was also most painfully knowledgeable of. However, for Willoughby to be so base as to force a woman he professed to love, though sadly believable, was not something even Colonel Brandon would have readily suspected. Indeed, no person of polite company would ever stoop to assume such a thing capable of a man who walked among them; charming them all with his winsome ways and genteel conduct in society.

For Colonel Brandon, his course was set, his conscious sure. The instant Marianne had confessed the wretched truth; that her child was conceived not only out of wedlock, but also through violence, he knew what Willoughby's fate would be. It only required a time and place. Such were his thoughts as he rested against the chamber door, trying to still his racing heart.

Elinor came upon him there after breakfast had ended, seeking Marianne's rooms in the hopes of being useful. Though sleeves and jacket had been restored to their proper place on the Colonel's person, there was something unusual about him that appeared almost dishevelled in his look and expression.

Fearing that it meant grave news about Marianne, she asked, "How does she fare, Colonel?"

"There is no reason for alarm," he said, putting her slightly at ease. "It is an ugly wound, but one that will heal quickly. The same prognosis cannot be given for the deeper pain that Mr. Willoughby has inflicted." He pronounced the man's title as if the very mention was a curse upon his lips. "Do take care of her, Miss Dashwood. I do not think even you can know what she is suffering at present."

Elinor blanched, misinterpreting his implication. "Do you mean that she has harmed herself deliberately?"

Colonel Brandon reassured her with a sad smile. "It is not what you imagine. I would, however, be most grateful to you if you would remain with us— permanently, if your mother can spare you. It would be a great comfort to know that she will not want for company when I am away, and I'm certain she would rather you be near her than I."

Elinor hurried to defend him. "Do not disparage yourself, Colonel. Your care of her does not go unnoticed. Marianne is still young at heart, and she can be distracted from the attention of others by the violence of her own feelings."

"I am sensible of that, but you mistake your sister if you think she has not on expressed her gratitude to me in frequent and varying ways. However, thankfulness and affection are not one in the same, and I would have her most in company and looked after by those she loves. I can think of none better than you."

Elinor could not argue the point, and so she left it be for the time. "Thank you, Colonel. Of course I will stay with her as long as she would wish it."

He answered with a slight inclination of the head and left her then. Elinor wondered at the cause of his weary gait and distressed features if Marianne's injury was not so very serious. Had she injured him by some thoughtless comment? It was not something beyond the usual for Marianne to unwittingly wound another in the throes of her despair.

Upon entering the room, Elinor found her sister reclining comfortably on the bed, looking no more pale or tired than the previous day, though no less, either.

"Oh, Elinor!" She put her hands out to receive her and to urge her to sit beside her on the bed. "I have been so foolish!"

"Are you badly hurt, dear? The Colonel tells me it is not a serious injury, but he seemed more perturbed than usual. Is it more than your arm that pains you?" When Marianne was reluctant to answer, Elinor went on, "I know how tiresome the journey from London was, and you are not fully recovered from the anxiety of the past fortnight."

"Not in body, no, but I've embarrassed myself this morning," Marianne sighed. "I had hoped to begin my marriage with industry, and instead... I feel so troublesome!"

Elinor hid a smile at this new turn of phrase from Marianne. She could not recall a time Marianne had ever admitted being troublesome before. "Colonel Brandon was most concerned when the housekeeper told him that you'd been injured. He pushed away from the table in such haste that he upset his breakfast plate and startled all the footmen."

"It is not so dreadful," Marianne said, failing to catch Elinor's point. "I only caused an issue with my ignorance. I will tell you everything, but you must promise not to laugh too much at me, or I might never recover."

Elinor could only promise that if it was something that caused Marianne true pain or embarrassment, she would not find it amusing. They made a silent agreement to cease conversation while the maid brought in a tray laden with a full breakfast, and a few delicacies of such exquisite taste that they brought unbidden tears to Marianne's eyes. "Elinor," she murmured, "he is so good to me; so very kind and good, and I do not deserve it."

"He loves you, Marianne. In his eyes you could not be more deserving of his kindness."

Marianne sighed deeply at this pronouncement, long suspected, but never fully confessed. "I had thought love to be all fervent passion, shown by romantic verse and with unsuppressed remonstrance. But I was wrong, Elinor. I've been wrong about Colonel Brandon in so many ways." She finished swallowing her tea, the better to replace her cup with Elinor's hand. "He says you may stay with us as long as I desire you near me, Elinor! And once I am well, you must help me learn how to be a good mistress of the house, and how the Colonel would like things, for I wish to repay him in whatever way I can for all that he's taken upon himself in marrying me."

"I do believe that asking the Colonel directly would be the best way to determine his preferences, but I will help you however I can, dear."

Elinor moved the breakfast tray aside, Marianne having taken her fill, and resumed her place on the bed. "I have written to Mama," she said.

"Oh, dear Mama," Marianne cried. "I should write to her once I feel a little better. I feared I'd not to see her again for the greater part of a year, and would need to invent some story to justify my absence. Now the only disappointment I must get over is that she was not able to attend the wedding. What did you write her?"

"I wrote of your marriage, explaining that you took Willoughby's engagement very badly; that you came to see how deceived you were in him, and that the Colonel's kindness through your trial turned your heart in acceptance of his offer. I'm certain she will believe it of you to be persuaded by the Colonel how for travelling purposes it was best to marry the sooner."

"Oh," Marianne exclaimed, "but I have always so ardently protested such inconstancies of affection! She will think me absurd!"

"Better that than a used woman, dearest," came Elinor's serious reminder.

The harshness of her sister's words, though not delivered in a deliberately cruel manner, struck Marianne's tender feelings and she began to cry.

"Oh, forgive me, dearest," Elinor soothed, "I did not mean to..."

"No, you are right. She had better think me flighty than degraded; and Mama has always been fond of the Colonel. I do not think she will be too disappointed," she comforted herself by musing.

"No, Marianne, there is no danger of her being disappointed in your husband."

Marianne continued, not recognising the irony in Elinor's tone. "In fact, if we had not met Edward first, and if Willoughby had not come upon me and turned my head, I think Mama would have liked Colonel Brandon for you, Elinor."

Elinor said nothing in reply to this remark, but chose to alight on a new subject.

"If you would like, I can bring paper and ink and write to Mama for you by dictation. Then your correspondence need not be delayed, and you will still be in accordance with your husband's orders to rest."

Marianne immediately brightened, and sent Elinor on with all haste to gather the materials suggested.

Following her letter, Elinor spent the remainder of the day touring the estate and gathering all manner of pertinent information to convey to

Marianne that she might better equip her for all the duties of managing such a household.

Colonel Brandon was a thoughtful and meticulous master, and his estate was well seen to even in his absences through his clear direction and the dutiful character of the housekeeper and head butler. There was not a great deal for Marianne to oversee, excepting some trifles that were more a matter of taste or ornamentation than household efficiency, nor was her interference greatly desired by the aforementioned staff.

The grounds were especially well tended, and though too cultivated perhaps for Marianne's pleasure, Elinor found great satisfaction in exploring the gardens and lawn.

Elinor could tell from their conversation, though not directly expressed by Marianne, that she still saw the Colonel as a kindly relation rather than a husband and lover, and though wholly done away with any lingering feelings for Willoughby she would not quickly be moved to love another no matter his worth.

She prayed that it might not be long; that Marianne's gratitude and unwavering interest in repaying the Colonel for his kindness might someday flourish into a deeper affection, and the constancy and faithfulness of the Colonel's love might finally be rewarded by Marianne's in turn.

Chapter Eight

"Mrs. Brandon, I hoped I might join you for tea this morning."

The request caught the recipient quite by surprise to the extent that she took her time in forming a response. In their full week of marriage, Colonel Brandon had never asked anything of Marianne, though she was always at the ready in case of any request, be it regarding action or inaction.

They had slipped into a daily routine that although not wholly unpleasant, was somewhat stunted by their self-enforced formality. In the past, such a suppression of true feeling would have stifled Marianne to the point of volatile frustration, but in her changed state she was content, if not perfectly happy, to do what she thought might please the Colonel in her quiet, unobtrusive existence. She rose late, wandered the grounds on Elinor's arm, made regular use of the grand instrument in the music room, and helped herself to whatever handsome volume in the library so delighted her to read at the time, all by encouragement of the Colonel, though never in his company.

In turn, Colonel Brandon was under the false impression that the greatest good he could do Marianne was to stay as far out of her way as possible, and with their combined misunderstandings, Marianne had begun to believe that despite his early attentions to her, he did not desire her company after all, and so the two were rarely together except in the evenings, when they took their meals with Elinor, and after dressing in separate rooms rejoined one another by sharing a bed, but with so much distance between them they might as well have been on opposite banks of the Thames.

In the morning, the Colonel had always slipped away so early and quietly that Marianne was never conscious of his departure, but awoke in solitude, and had formed a habit of taking her late breakfast while comfortably situated in her morning gown rather than taking the time to fully dress and delay breakfast for her sister and husband downstairs.

This morning, however, she had risen at a more reasonable hour, and was appropriately outfitted when her husband preceded the tea tray's arrival, asking if they might partake together.

Afraid he might misinterpret her hesitation for something other than mere surprise, she quickly rose to receive him, uncertain of how best to do so; whether it would be strange for her to offer him a seat in his own chambers, or if once past the threshold he might take up mastery of his suite again. "Of course, Colonel," she smiled warmly, clasping his hands in welcome, and then hastening to the tea service in a flutter of confusion as an unexpected flush added colour to her cheeks.

The nature of his expression upon being accepted in such a way did not escape Marianne's attention. It was equal parts relief and surprise, as if he'd been thoroughly expectant of being sent away directly. The tenderness of his features softened him so that Marianne thought him rather youthful for the short duration of his smile. When he was not so grave and his appearance less troubled, she thought he could easily pass for a man not so very far from a proper marrying age.

"These are your apartments," she reminded him, humour in her tone. "You need not ask to spend your time here."

"I do not wish to intrude," he said.

"Intrude on your wife?" She supposed in former times she had treated the Colonel's presence as an intrusion, and it was no wonder he was unaware of a change of sentiment in her that had never been expressed. "I believe you take your tea plain?" she said by way of distraction, feeling shamed at her previous behaviour.

"I thank you, yes."

Marianne fulfilled the prescriptions of her own indulgent tea and brought her cup along with his as she joined him on the couch. Not one for prolonged silences when there was clearly a subject to light upon, Marianne began by prompting, "May I ask what manner of topic has risked this so called 'intrusion?'"

Colonel Brandon was perched stiffly at the end of the couch, no less distant than he might have been before their marriage, and much further than

Willoughby had ever endured to be from the object of *his* desire. It was with another blush that Marianne recalled the last time she and the Colonel had sat here together, and how it had ended with her leaning on his shoulder and encompassed in his arms.

"I wished to speak of your mother's impending arrival," he said, holding both teacup and saucer, but not drinking. "I am told that she is to be kept ignorant of the true nature of our marriage, but I am certain it would ease her mind to see that you are settled comfortably in your new home. In the interest therefore of her finding you thus, I beg that you tell me if there is anything I might do to further your happiness here."

"Dear Colonel," she said with a laugh, astonishing herself as much as him in the sincerity of her phrasing, "I cannot imagine you doing any more to secure my comfort than you already have."

His relief was evidenced by the way he let his shoulders lose some of their tension and he took a brisk sip of tea, partially in satisfaction, and partially in delayed recovery over Marianne's 'dear Colonel.'

"Except... perhaps..." she began haltingly. His gaze was instantly fixed on her and the tea set aside, ready at once to put to rights whatever she found amiss. "We see so very little of each other," she frowned, "and as my mother knows me all too well, I fear she'll become immediately suspicious if I am not as comfortable with the master of Delaford as I am with the estate itself. Could we not... spend more time in one another's company? It seems a natural occurrence in any good marriage for a husband's business to intrude on his wife's affairs, and though it is not in my nature to pretend an interest in things which do not seize my fascination," she openly admitted, "I am interested in knowing you better, Colonel."

"Me?" he echoed with some alarm.

"Yes, Colonel, you. I wish to know the man I have married. What are your passions, your pursuits, your purpose? I find so many books on your shelves that speak of similar tastes to my own, and it is the same with the music you've given me to learn, but I have no way of confirming or disproving my ideas of you. There must be somewhere we could begin more naturally."

"I am not well practiced in the arts of polite conversation," he warned, though not unkindly.

"Nor am I, I'm afraid. But I since have the unhappy disposition of speaking a great deal too much of my own opinion, and if it is your nature to speak too little, perhaps we may help each other," she offered. "Shall we... take tea together every morning like we are now? Provided you are not obligated to attend another appointment?"

He inclined his head, the youthful smile returning to his face, making him almost... handsome, she thought. "I confess such an arrangement is exactly what I might wish, if you can bear the prolonged company of such an ancient relic as I."

Having considered the matter settled in the good-natured smiles that passed between them at his teasing, Marianne took opportunity in starting at once. She found it easier than suspected to pique the Colonel's interest by simply speaking of her own likes and dislikes, and discovered him full of insight and sentiments cultivated not only through diligent study, but worldly experience. He knew so much on such a diversity of subjects that were it not for his agreeable manner it might have put Marianne in too much awe of him to proceed comfortably. They descended to breakfast together that morning, and had become not only easy with each other in the interim, but merry, each in their own way.

Elinor regarded it in the healthy colour that had returned to Marianne's cheeks as she took her chair, and the cheerful gait and nod of greeting from the Colonel. She saw these marked changes, but kept them as observations to herself, not desiring to spoil the easiness of the breakfast table with her own private joy, in case it caused embarrassment to either party.

It was on the morning of her mother's arrival that Marianne first began to notice that the gowns which had fit so poorly due to her ill health were now snug in places she thought rather strange. Elinor gently reminded her that it was not solely the overindulgence of Colonel Brandon's breakfast table that made her so, but the condition she was in was certain to bring even more changes upon her that she would not so easily hide in the coming months.

The thought gave Marianne a cause for brief panic, but as she was not visibly rounder in ways that simple tucks and cinching could not conceal, the alarm was put aside for the receiving of their mother and Margaret.

The two missing elements of the family followed

their invitation to stay at Delaford post-haste, and Mrs. Dashwood was gathering her favourite daughter into her arms almost before Marianne was sufficiently prepared. Mrs. Dashwood blessedly mistook all of her fierce blushing for a newlywed glow, and her determination to discuss in great detail every matter *besides* her sudden marriage was assumed to be embarrassment at having fallen so quickly in love with a man she used to deride as quite aged, though being no more than five and thirty. It was therefore a pleasant beginning with Marianne's anxiety concerning her mother so quickly abated, and Margaret as a diversion for introducing any number of topics Marianne counted safe.

Supposing that she would not always have Elinor to assist her — for Marianne was not shaken in her resolve to have her married to Edward — Marianne had begun to manage the household on her own; little things at the first, but gradually and surely she took a more prominent role, allowing Elinor to slip into her natural position as a guest, and her mother to be receive in like manner. She was now able to give tours of the house with only a little floundering at certain turns or in dimly lighted corridors, but it was not so much the direction of things that eluded her, but the placement of small yet significant objects that had always been in Elinor's care before.

It was in such a moment of searching — the larder keys being temporarily misplaced — that she came across a most singular sight. In the private library — a smaller room than the grand library where the Colonel had squirreled away some of his favourite books, and taken no pains to arrange furniture in a manner suiting anyone but himself — she found him in full dress, reclining comfortably in a large, leather chair, boots upon the ottoman, reading prose aloud to his two dogs.

She watched and listened for some time, her presence being betrayed at last by the lively Dalmatian perking her head up and trembling all over with enthusiasm at the prospect of more active pursuits. One word from her master was enough to keep her from bounding towards Marianne in welcome, but the damage had been done, and the Colonel started and coloured slightly when he turned in his chair to see what had excited her so.

"Oh!" Marianne cried, "Do not stop on my account!" She hastened to the chair opposite him, the better to reach the more subdued of his dogs who liked to put his nose in her hand while she pet him, and also to prevent Colonel Brandon from moving from his own seat to stand at her coming. "That was beautiful! Do you often read to your dogs?"

"I find it helps to settle them after a chase, and for me to hear the words spoken aloud, as I believe verse was meant to be enjoyed."

"Will you continue, then? Would you object to reading to me, as well?" she asked delighted. "And to... to...?" she hesitated, not being familiar with his dogs' names.

"Duke is the doting one with his head currently in your lap, and Molly there would rather not take a rest for poetry, but run herself into exhaustion."

"And will you read to us?" Marianne persisted.

That half-formed, but meaningful smile crept over his lips and he nodded once his acquiescence. "If you can bear to listen."

"I have never denied your gift for reading, Colonel. It is Edward I despair of."

This new discovery of the Colonel's pastime afforded Marianne yet another way to while the hours in the pursuit of better knowing her husband. It became her favourite part of the day, when they would take their places by the fire, and Duke and Molly too, to hear the Colonel read to them. Elinor was invited as well, but often excused herself with exaggerated trifles or errands with their mother and Margaret so that they might have their time alone. Alone, that is, besides the two loving giants that sat at Marianne's feet, and by whose acceptance was perhaps the strongest affirmation to her truly being the mistress of Delaford.

Chapter Nine

The weight of Elinor's disappointment in love was considerably lessened by her sister's marital happiness, as was her removal from the company of Lucy Steele and her odious badgering, though her disappointment was not so forgotten that she was able to be perfectly content all her waking hours. She had a number of pursuits to keep her occupied however, as her correspondence had extended beyond her mother's to include Mrs. Jennings, and through no will of her own, that very Lucy Steele whom she had been so fortunate as to part ways with. The sudden marriage of the Colonel and Marianne had caused quite the stir amongst the ladies in Mrs. Jennings' company, and the news had circulated in London and without with fascinating rapidity.

Elinor took care in returning Mrs. Jennings' spirited congratulations — which was not without some self-congratulatory sentiments for promoting the match herself — with a letter of thanks in regard to her generosity in thinking of the sisters and her hospitality in housing them during their brief stay in London.

Lucy's letter was not half so agreeable in either the reading of or the responding to. Her platitudes of friendship were no more sincere than her well-wishes for Marianne. She even alluded to the fact that marriages formed in such haste were generally to hide some scandal or other, through which tones Elinor could only infer that she was jealous over Marianne's immediate securing of a husband while Lucy was still enduring a secret engagement. Of that, Lucy wrote at length; the contents of her letter predominately taken over by how often 'Mr. F.' wrote to her, and how delightful she found Mrs. Ferrars—who though she considered of a very severe countenance and disposition, was surely the kindest of ladies at heart—and she had every hope of securing the family's approval of the match in just a week longer of such affable fellowship, reminding Elinor to dispose of her letter just as soon as it was read, lest the contents be discovered by anyone else, for she trusted no one half so well as her dear Miss Dashwood. Indeed, Miss Dashwood was quite her favourite, and she made certain she was aware of it by peppering her letter with addresses to her, using her title, "my dear Miss Dashwood" as often as was possible on two full sheets of paper.

It pained Elinor to reply to such a missive in the first place, but obligated by courtesy, she managed to form a satisfactory number of lines that were neither unkind, nor untruthful. She answered Lucy's foolish exaggerations with sensible commentary, and her ignorant suppositions with verified facts, but wrote nothing that would give indication of how thoroughly bruised she was by maintaining such a correspondence. Even her warning that Mrs. Ferrars's acceptance of Lucy might well be attributed to the fact that she was in complete ignorance of Lucy's relation to her son was composed with no malice whatsoever.

Besides letter writing, Elinor had her mother and youngest sister to entertain as well. They required very little in the way of diversions, as Margaret was as captivated by Colonel Brandon's library as Marianne had been, albeit her enjoyment being derived from a very different sort of book collection, and Mrs. Dashwood was content to take her needlework to any cheerful spot in the great house and spend her days in a leisurely way—save for her worrying over Elinor's chance at matrimony, now that Marianne was settled so well.

Thankfully, Elinor could persuade her out of such topics with very little effort if she only turned the conversation to her favourite daughter.

"Dear Marianne!" Mrs. Dashwood would exclaim, sufficiently distracted, a bright smile captivating her features as if she was even now witnessing the union between her daughter and Colonel Brandon before her very eyes. "Do they not make a handsome couple, Elinor? He is so stately, and she is so beautiful. I was disappointed at first that they married so quickly, and without first receiving my consent. Of course the Colonel is an honourable man, and how could I ever have denied them?—but could you not have persuaded her to postpone the wedding until she might have had my blessing?" To Elinor's relief, her mother did not truly expect an answer and so continued without pause. "Well, I've had my apology from Colonel Brandon, and there was nothing amiss in it, so I am not at all unhappy how things came about. I suppose she was eager to be over the disappointment with Willoughby, my poor girl. In truth, I can understand her haste to have her name cease to be coupled with his. There was always something, you remember, in Willoughby's eyes I did not like." Elinor only smiled to herself knowingly at that, but Mrs. Dashwood did not pause in either her speech or her sewing, carrying on her conversation as she pulled a new stitch through her work. "The Colonel may not be as romantic a husband as Marianne once dreamed, but he is every bit deserving of her. And she has grown so healthy and of such fine form since you left. Do not you think so?"

Elinor did think so, and what's more she was afraid that Marianne's "healthy" condition might begin to show in less concealable ways before much longer. It was therefore soon after that she made a bid for returning to Barton Cottage. She appealed for the sake of Marianne establishing herself more thoroughly as mistress of the house and perhaps to force her into closer relations with her husband if she did not have Elinor there to fall back on for company, though her greater motive was to give Mrs. Dashwood and Margaret reason to quit the house before Marianne was grown round with child and her gowns would not be made to hide it. Mrs. Dashwood agreed under the persuasive sentiment that they must not intrude on the Colonel's good will any longer, and preparations for departure were begun.

Before arrangements could be fully formed for their removal, a letter arrived again, bearing cruel tidings for Elinor by the hand of that social informant Mrs. Jennings. The engagement that she had been burdened with the knowledge of was now out for all the world to know, or rather, all the family, friends, and acquaintances of the Dashwoods, Steeles, and Ferrarses combined, which might as well contain the whole of the British Commonwealth. The elder Miss Steele had let a careless comment slip about their previous acquaintance with Edward Ferrars, and with one or two interrogative measures from Fanny and Mrs. Dashwood, she had related the whole of the story to them both. The end result, after the initial shock, revulsion, and horror, had been for Mrs. Ferrars to throw both the Miss Steeles out of the house, and disinherit Edward upon his refusal to break his promise. She irrevocably settled the entire inheritance on Mr. Robert Ferrars and gave Lucy such a scolding before sending her away as to bring her to hysteria. There were not more particulars, for Mrs. Jennings had not waited for the outcome in order to write a more succinct and accurate letter, but had rather chosen to rely on sensation to convey her message. There were also a few hasty lines expressing her embarrassment in once teasing Elinor about that 'Mr. F,' and she was very shocked and sorry indeed, but she had never expected such a turn-about, and after this, nothing should surprise her again.

Elinor thought she had best tell Marianne before she heard word of it from another. Though it was not very likely word would reach her soon as news from the outside world was predominately conveyed to her through Elinor's letter writing and the Colonel's conversations, it did not seem fair to keep her in the dark while the whole of the ton were speaking of it and such near relations were involved.

Marianne was utterly confounded and at first did not believe it, supposing Mrs. Jennings had mistaken Edward for his brother Robert or some such folly.

"I'm afraid it is all perfectly true," Elinor said with a great deal more composure than she felt. They sat together in Elinor's room; a cheerful, sunny place with windows facing east, which afforded a great deal of light in the mornings by which she did her letter writing. Today, however, there seemed a dark pallor over the room, and it was not just from the gloomy weather. "Lucy told me in no uncertain terms that she has been engaged to Edward Ferrars these past four years—five, as it is now. I could be no more certain unless Edward himself had told me."

"All this time I have been making you a couple in my mind!" Marianne cried indignantly. "Why did you not tell me? And for how long have you known this?" she asked a little crossly.

"These four months I have known the whole of their history, forced upon me by Lucy when we had known her no more than a week," Elinor admitted, still bravely composed, though tears had begun to tease at her eyes and she attempted to hide them by fixing her gaze away from Marianne's searching looks. "It was told to me in the strictest of confidences and I could not break my word. And what might you have done with such information? Would it have made any difference?"

"I may not have come to London," Marianne frowned, troubled greatly by the duration of her ignorance.

"And then we would have been miles away from the Colonel, and you would have had no salvation from your fate. No, Marianne. It is good we came, if only for that reason." She tried to console her sister with a sad, unconvincing smile. "Do not be cross with me for concealing it, Marianne. I was no more happy in keeping such a secret as you can be to find it out."

At this petition, Marianne took Elinor's hand in both of hers and held it to her cheek. "Poor, unhappy Elinor. I am not cross with you. What you must have been suffering all this while. How could you bear it?" she wondered. "How could you ever remain silent through all the intolerable jests of Mrs. Jennings?"

"Her remarks I well could have borne, were it not for the constant pestering of Lucy Steele in my ear of how deep an affection she and Edward feel for one another. Oh, Marianne," she said sorrowfully, emotions growing tender over her sister's tearful concern, "I am glad that you know now, and I need not hide my disappointment to you at least."

"But he does not love her, Elinor! How could he possibly? Tell me if you saw anything in Lucy's character or conversation to support such a notion, and I shall try to believe it. But she seems to me such a ridiculous, insufferable ninny with no sense of feeling whatever! And even if she were not so bad as I perceive her, I know he loves *you*," she insisted. "He cannot marry her!"

"Would you have him prove himself dishonourable in casting her off as Willoughby has done to you?"

"Our situations are hardly the same, Elinor," Marianne said with a biting tone. "And I would not have him act against his conscience, but neither would I have him marry where he does not love! He does not love her!" she repeated.

"Perhaps," Elinor began in Edward's defence, "he does harbour some... regret over the engagement, but it was a promise made long before he met me and he has honoured it admirably. He has made me no overtures, offered me no more than friendship, and he did try to tell me of Lucy on several occasions, though I believe the right words escaped him. I do believe he will be happy in the knowledge that he did his duty and kept his word. After all," she sighed in resignation, "After all that is bewitching about the idea of one's happiness depending entirely on one person, it is not always possible, we must accept. Edward will marry Lucy, and I shall go home with Mama."

"Always resignation and acceptance," Marianne spoke tearfully. "Always honour, and prudence, and duty."

"Elinor," she said, cupping her cheeks in a nearly motherly fashion, "Does your heart not tell you otherwise? Or perhaps you did not love him so very much after all." This last was expressed with a gentle sigh, as if it were a great comfort to think it was so.

At this, Elinor started back as if struck with a physical blow and she rose from her seat beside Marianne. "What do you know of my heart? For weeks, I have had this pressing on my heart and mind without being at liberty to speak of it to a single creature while you were suffering all the while over Willoughby." She pressed a hand to her heart in suppressed emotion, her voice wavering as she went on. "I have had to remain cheerful, and careful, unable to speak a word of my own disappointment while your pain was foremost, even recognised by Mrs. Jennings and the very person whose prior claims ruined all my hope." Her breath caught as she took a chair away from Marianne to steady herself. "I have endured Lucy's exultation again and again whilst knowing myself to be divided from Edward forever. Believe me, Marianne, had I not been bound to silence I could have produced enough evidence of a broken heart for even you to believe how unhappy I have been."

"Oh, Elinor!" Marianne began to weep openly, and this caused Elinor reason to compose herself once more. She removed from her solitary chair to embrace Marianne in acceptance of her broken apology. "I have been so mistaken in others," she wept. "I did not understand the Colonel's sincerity, and I have not understood your heart. I have been wretchedly selfish, and I will learn to do better! But, Elinor," she said, drying her eyes the better to face her sister, "I cannot agree with you entirely in defending Edward. Perhaps he is acting honourably from the position of strict moral duty, but it is hardly honourable to his heart. No," she shook her head decidedly. "I will always believe that Edward loved you, that he still loves you! For how could he not?!"

Touched as she was by Marianne's loving outbursts, Elinor was weary of the topic and wished to escape a conversation that could do no more good than harm if it were to continue. "Let's speak no more of it, dearest," she requested, a weary breath being the greatest sign of her inner turmoil, now that her tears were at an end.

Marianne agreed, and the remainder of their interlude consisted of making any evidence of their tearful exchange disappear and conversing on matters that could only produce cheerfulness. But it was as early as the same evening that Elinor would be made to hear of it again, even with their mother kept in the dark, so that she would have no opportunity to cast further shadows of gloom upon their already downcast moods.

It was not Mrs. Dashwood, but Colonel Brandon who gave opportunity for the subject, and in a way that brought Elinor much undeserved distress, though of course he could not know how his desire to be useful increased her suffering.

They were assembled in the drawing room; the three of them spending a cosy evening in conversation as was now their usual way. Mrs. Dashwood had retired early with Margaret and Elinor might have done the same, but she wished to take advantage of the few nights remaining at Delaford by being near Marianne. Molly's rambunctious antics were kept at bay by the Colonel's careful watch, but he was not as strict with her as usual, nor did he take such a passive role in the conversation.

Upon a lull in one of Marianne's impassioned speeches regarding a lesser known poet, he offered his acquired information. "Ah. I have it through Sir John Middleton that your friend, Edward Ferrars is to be married to Miss Lucy Steele."

Marianne glanced at Elinor and opened her mouth with an indignant retort on her lips, but a fierce look of warning from Elinor stopped her.

"It is true," Elinor answered. "I have had the same information from Mrs. Jennings who gave me a thorough account of the matter."

Colonel Brandon accepted this confirmation with a tight frown. "I think it is reprehensible how the family has reacted." At this, Marianne looked up at him in surprise. "I know all too well the cruelties of a family's exclusion of a young couple desirous of marriage." His eyes sought Marianne's for the briefest of moments, and she determined to ask him for particulars of his own history, as it was evident he spoke from personal experience.

"I have thought of something that may help them, though," Colonel Brandon continued. "I am told he is seeking a profession in the clergy. The living at Delaford is recently made vacant and I thought to offer it to him."

"Colonel," Elinor said quickly, disallowing Marianne from bursting out in protestation, "That is exceedingly generous of you."

"It is a small parsonage in need of some repairs, but it is comfortable, I think, and it would allow them to marry despite the unkindness of his nearest relations. Would you accompany me tomorrow in looking over the property and pointing out what improvements might be necessary for them? As Mr. Ferrars's friend and an acquaintance of Miss Lucy Steele, I would desire your counsel in manner of the proceedings."

"I... Colonel, you give me more credit than I think is due. Should you not rather rely on your own judgement in what is profitable for your estate?"

"I think not. I have every confidence that you will be able to direct those feminine alterations which my eyes may dismiss." He turned his attention to Marianne. "If you are feeling up to a little walking, I will have the carriage bring you to the parish and we will all survey the property together."

Marianne was undergoing such a conflict of emotions that it was impossible for her to form a reply. Her gaze darted from Elinor to the Colonel and back to Elinor. She did not want to hurt the Colonel in appearing reluctant, but she was painfully aware of all she had discovered of Elinor's sentiments during their morning conversation, and wanted more than anything to relieve some of her burden.

Finally, she was able to provide a diplomatic answer, though it took some effort. "I am feeling up to anything that will help Elinor. If that means accompanying you to the parish, then I shall."

Elinor rewarded her with a thankful smile, and though Marianne knew she was not really happy, nor could she be in such circumstances, it was a genuine smile that went straight to her sister's heart.

Chapter Ten

Marianne could not stay still over Colonel Brandon's offer of a living to Edward. She told Elinor as much in no uncertain terms, declaring the whole thing preposterous and insisting she would ask her husband to reconsider before the invitation could be drafted. Elinor begged that she say nothing to the Colonel regarding the truth of her affections lest he regret his decision, and ruin Edward's chances of a comfortable living with the woman he'd promised to marry.

Marianne still did not agree, nor did she bind herself to complete secrecy, though she did assure Elinor that she would hold her tongue for the duration of their viewing the property Edward and Lucy were to live in, should the Colonel's generosity come to fruition.

Though she remained true to her word in making no open remark against the future tenants of her husband's property, Marianne was hardly enthused and she was rather unhelpful in the overseeing of repairs and improvements. Everything was, "suitable enough for them," she was sure, and had especially sharp comments to make against the intended parishioner's wife, doubting her ability to appreciate any improvements whatever, considering the extent of her education. She did not realise that her sarcasm only pained Elinor more than a sullen silence would have, but she was unable to forebear such a turn of events with patience, and Elinor did not blame her too much for the way she showed her displeasure. For she knew it was for her sake and the sympathy Marianne felt for her unattainable love that drove her to such obvious unkindness, and though it was not the most gracious way of making her sentiments known, it was Marianne's way, and evidenced her deep affection for Elinor.

The Colonel was not without perception, and at the end of the evening, when he joined his wife in their shared chamber, he took opportunity of asking her if she was quite well. Marianne was still in a state of frenzied upset and had been moving about the room, rearranging all that she put her hands on, never finding a satisfactory position for either articles about the room or her own comfort in sitting. Her restlessness disallowed the Colonel to remove his robe and slip into bed unnoticed, and he was momentarily uncertain of how to proceed with this new development of a fully awake Marianne in nightgown and fast loosening braid, hurrying about the room with no conceivable purpose.

"I feared today's activities might have fatigued you, but you seem to be quite... energised," he wondered aloud in his confusion, not venturing any further than the corner of the room closest to his side of the great bed.

"No, I am not tired. I cannot be restful with such thoughts plaguing my mind as they are."

"Might you share with me what thoughts distress you so?"

Marianne set down a gilded trinket box, perhaps with a little more force than necessary, and heaved a deep sigh. "I am not supposed to tell, but it is very trying not to be able to explain to you the reason for my vexation, since you are the one unwittingly causing it."

"If you are unable to speak of it first, allow me to hazard a guess," he offered. "Are you displeased with my decision to offer Edward the parish here? Would you rather I consulted you, first?" he queried, barely missing the mark, "I had thought him a good friend of your family."

"Yes, Edward is a dear friend, and I think him worthy of every possible comfort in his future. That is why," she began vehemently, stopping short when her words threatened to betray Elinor. "But no, I am sorry. You musn't misunderstand. It is not that you offer such a thing that distresses me, or even that it is for Edward's sake. I think it the best and most generous of solutions, were it not for... for who he brings here as wife."

"Do you have some quarrel with Miss Lucy Steele?"

Marianne repeated her sigh, but with less fervour. "Only that it is her attachment to Edward which will trap him forever in a loveless marriage. I am well aware that Edward does his duty, but I am even more aware that he does not love her! True, he is of a tender-hearted and kindly nature, and will give every impression of being perfectly content with his small income and his ridiculous wife. But to love such a superior creature as he does and then be made to marry Lucy Steele for the sake of honour! Can the heart truly be content to perpetuate such insincerity, such lack of real passion? How is it to be borne?! Poor Edward!" she lamented. "Poor Eli..." she was about to say her sister's name, but remembered to hold her tongue and sank defeated on the bed rather than finish her exclamation.

Colonel Brandon was quiet for a moment. Marianne sat with her back to him and he could not ascertain her meaning by way of expression. Then his voice carried in a low, downcast manner from across the room, "Are those your own sentiments? Do you feel trapped in a loveless marriage, forced into it as you were for the sake of honour?"

"Oh!" she cried, twisting about to see the disappointed furrow in his brow. "I did not mean..."

Colonel Brandon attempted a sad smile of understanding. "I do not wish to further your distress. Perhaps you would be more comfortable if we slept in separate chambers from now on. There is no more danger of suspicion being cast upon your character."

He was turning to leave, but Marianne rose and rushed to his side with surprising agility despite her condition, grasping the sleeve of his robe before he could go.

"Colonel, please! I made no allusion to my own sentiments; I spoke only of Edward's plight! I assure you, I do not feel trapped or stifled by any means. You are all kindness, and sympathy, and I am not ignorant of how... how fond you are of me," she stammered, colouring slightly. "Do not take my words to heart, please. I am only grieved for my friend, as I know him to be in love with another."

Unconvinced, he went on, "You have said yourself that you cannot imagine a life of polite contentment to be either a fulfilling or happy one. You see me as very old and unsuitable a husband, I know, and I cannot in good faith argue with you on such matters, being that you know your own heart better than anyone."

"Perhaps I do not know my own heart so well after all," she countered, tightening her grip on the sleeve so that he might not turn away again. "I have been wrong in a great many things of late, not the least of which is all that I ever said against you as a suitor. I know... I know you have given me so much, and though it is abominably selfish, I would ask one more favour of you, Colonel. Do not give up hope. My heart is yet sore and bruised, and I struggle to reconcile my feelings now with what they were before our marriage, but I am not as stupid as I once was." She let her hand fall from its insistent grasp, dropping into his and giving it a gentle squeeze. "I do not think you are very old, nor unsuitable," she assured him with a real smile. Then, daring to rise on her toes, she brushed a gentle kiss upon his cheek to confirm the truth of her words. "Will you forgive me, Colonel, and come to bed? Your presence here does not distress me in the least."

Considering the matter settled by the fact that he no longer attempted to make his exit from the room, Marianne prepared to return to her place on the bed, but Colonel Brandon could not let her go without giving her an answer in like kind by raising her hand to his lips.

As they settled into bed, both far too conscious of what had just passed between them to make conversation, Marianne felt the heat rise to her face as she divested her robe, though she had already slept many nights beside the Colonel in naught but her nightgown. It was so very different, climbing into bed together and after having kissed, though their lips had never met. It suddenly seemed a very intimate thing they were doing, and she wondered that it would cause such palpitations of the heart and flushed cheeks when there was surely nothing shameful in sharing a bed with her husband.

After laying in utter silence for what seemed an eternity, Marianne could not help but ask rather abruptly, "Can you not rescind your offer?" She turned onto her side in order to make her request while looking the Colonel in the eye.

"If you wish it, I will," he said, slightly perturbed by her near proximity and pleading demeanour. "Though I feel it may cause the woman he loves even more pain to know both Mr. Ferrars and his new wife will suffer for it."

Marianne nodded, causing her braid to fall against her shoulder that was now free of any material since her robe had been removed and her shift had fallen enticingly past any modest situation. Colonel Brandon attempted to focus on her words rather than his desire to brush his fingers against the softness of her shoulder upon the excuse of moving her braid.

"I know it is wrong," she said sleepily, stifling a yawn. "I only wish something could be done for poor, dear Elinor."

The Colonel made no comment on her revelation that Elinor was indeed the woman Edward truly loved, and in Marianne's tiredness, she did not seem to consider that what she'd given away was of any great significance.

"She does love him terribly," she murmured, no longer meeting the Colonel's gaze. "Even if she is too prudent to let it show."

"I think I may know something of your sister's sentiments," he answered quietly and with profound meaning, but Marianne had already succumbed to sleep.

She rose the next morning to discover herself bereft of the Colonel's presence yet again. There was nothing unusual in it to cause alarm, yet something felt amiss in the quietness of the room, and the emptiness she felt from it. Her anxiety was confirmed by way of a letter she found on her dressing table; directed to her and in the Colonel's neat hand.

My Dearest Marianne,

You must forgive me for taking action once more without consulting you, but I could not be made aware of the violent crime Willoughby is guilty of without requiring satisfaction, and have challenged Mr. Willoughby to a duel. He has accepted my terms, and we meet in but a few hours of my penning this letter.

My true desire is to utterly dispense with him and rid the world of such a scoundrel, for were it possible I would do so with a clear conscience, as it is no secret how he despises his new wife, and she him. I would not, therefore, be leaving her without estate or income, and rather than depriving her of a protector, I should be relieving her of entrapment in one of those loveless marriages you so despise. The only regret I may have is if such a deed would cause you any heartache, but in light of your admission to me last night in the dissimilarity of situations, I believe I can safely trust that you would not think too harshly of my dismissal of the rogue.

It was not for his sake, however, that I did not make the terms to end with mortal blows, but the concern of what might come of you and your sister were I to be killed, instead. There is some small chance one of us may die, if the wounds inflicted are serious enough, but it is not my intent to leave you without a protector in this world, and it is not only that, but the knowledge that I am a superior swordsman that makes me eager rather than fearful to cross swords with Willoughby this morning.

If, by some sorry accident, I do succumb to death, you must allow me now to convey the great honour I have found in being your husband, short a time as it has been, and the gratitude I owe you for having made my last days on earth, if these are to be so, the most rewarding I have spent. Perhaps you are not aware how unchanged my affection for you has been since first meeting you at Barton Cottage. It has not only remained steadfast, but deepened as time has gone on, and that vengeful part of me is glad for the chance to repay Willoughby some of what I have suffered whilst apart from you. You are forever thanking me for doing you the great service of marrying you, yet I think it a disservice to me in misinterpreting my intentions. I had resolved to be as your sister has been in the face of unattainable love; patiently bearing suppressed affection without complaint *or breaking of trust, but I find it more and more impossible to hide from you the full depth of my affections.*

I am captivated by your very smile. I thrill over your very presence. You asked me not to relinquish all hope of your ever returning my love, and I cling to those words even as I prepare to meet the base creature who threatened to take from you all chance of future happiness.

I have written to Mr. Edward Ferrars as well, regarding the living I mean to offer him at Delaford in terms only as tempting as I feel my Christian duty, bearing the dilemma of your sister's heart in mind. I leave my unsent letter to him here for your approval. If all is well with my selection of phrasing, my seal is in the library, and you may direct and send it in my name.

I remain yours devotedly,

Col Brandon

This epistle was read once over in haste, then again at length, and once more when Marianne threatened to be overcome by emotions that rendered the words incomprehensible. When the full meaning of the letter was grasped, Marianne ran to her sister's room and burst through the door without precedent. "Oh, Elinor!' she cried, tears streaming down her cheek, and the letter crunching between her tightened fist. She was then astonished into silence by the sight of Elinor fully dressed and folding her gowns into a trunk.

"Oh! I had forgot you are leaving today!"

"Just as soon as we can adequately prepare. I think it best to be established again at Barton long before Edward and Lucy arrive. I have no wish for them to imagine I left on their account. But what is the matter, dearest? Who is that letter from? Is it not too early for the post?"

"It is from Colonel Brandon," Marianne said languidly.

"What on earth has happened? You look rather pale. Should you like to sit down?"

"Nothing!" she assured her, drying her eyes quickly. She did not tell Elinor of the Colonel's duel. She did not want to worry her into staying at Delaford longer after she had undergone such a day of heartache only the day previous. "No, I am fine. It is only... he had some business early this morning, and left me this to send to Edward," she said, extending the folded missive towards Elinor. "He says I am to direct it if it meets with my approval. Shall I send it?"

Elinor did not take it, but pushed the hand back towards her sister. "Of course you should send it, dearest. You know I think it the only course there is."

"Very well," Marianne murmured.

"Are you certain you are quite alright?" Elinor persisted.

"Yes, I am well." She collected herself with a cheerful tone and smile she did not feel. "The letter only startled me."

"It seems a very long letter only to ask your approval regarding Edward's living."

"It... it is a love letter, as well." Marianne blushed furiously.

"I see," Elinor said with a knowing smile, and Marianne was even more convinced not to speak a word of her husband's current whereabouts at the moment, or the way her heart raced near to bursting at the thought of him acquiring some mortal wound by Willoughby's hand. She feared not only worrying Elinor, but being unable to bear it should she be made to speak the words aloud.

"Shall I help you pack?" she asked without enthusiasm.

"If you like. Though you are not the most methodical and I may need to start all over again after you've been at it," Elinor teased.

Marianne forced a laugh. "Then I will leave you to it and see if Margaret would like my help. She is not so fastidious about her trunks."

Chapter Eleven

The minutes dragged on like hours for Marianne as soon as she'd watched the carriage roll out of the drive to take her mother and sisters away. She was sorry to see them go, but secretly relieved as well, wanting them nowhere near if Colonel Brandon was to arrive home injured or even worse, brought back killed after duelling Willoughby.

She had often considered what she might do all alone in such a great estate, but it had never been under the supposition that it would be whilst driven mad with worry over the possibility of becoming a young widow.

Every possible outcome of gruesome death or mortal injury played through her mind, causing directed employment impossible. The best she could do besides sitting and fretting was to visit Molly in the kennels and ask the master to let her take several romps around the grounds so that Marianne might follow at a brisk pace, pretending to ignore the fears that lay hold of her mind when she was not exercising her body in some fashion.

When Molly was returned to the kennels,

Marianne had nothing left to do but wait. Books could not hold her interest. The romantic prose and eloquent sonnets usually poignant with meaning and transporting her very soul by the pure felicity of genius were dulled by the reality she was suffering, and at their worst, even ridiculous in nature. The tragedies of unrequited love and untimely deaths mocked her, chided her, rebuked her, even, and she could not endure their sermonising as she waited for news of her husband.

She wandered listlessly through rooms, going from window to window in the hopes of catching sight or sound of the Colonel's horse approaching, appearing sometimes to be purposeful when encountering one of the servants, but otherwise aimless, and not caring how distracted she seemed.

She found it strange to be so alone; to be forced to imagine the halls and rooms without Colonel Brandon to ever step foot in them again. With a pang, she realised how truly bereft she would be to never again hear his slow and cautious step into the room she occupied; to never sit by the fire as he read aloud; to never again catch the loving and admiring smile he would give her when she played through a difficult measure, or referenced something he'd once told her of, or spoke any kind word in his favour.

It was in those agonising hours of loneliness that she came to know her own heart, and the place Colonel Brandon had in it. She did not think she could do without him, and it was not for the sake of the protection and support he so freely offered, but for his person that she grieved. Now that they had married, she would not be branded a loose woman once the child was born, and were she to return to her mother and sisters, they could live much as they always had, but with a small addition to their family. In marrying her, Colonel Brandon had given her a clean slate for the future, regardless of whom his estate was to be entailed to, and he had promised even so to take care of her.

But it was not the question of income that caused her head to ache, and her heart to race in an unsettled rhythm. She had grown sincerely fond of the Colonel, and did not have any desire to return to her mother's house, now that she'd been placed in the role of wife and mistress, and knew how pleasant it was to have her own home and husband. She loved their cottage, it was true. However, there was much to admire at Delaford Park that Barton could not boast. Not the least of which was its owner, Colonel Brandon.

Her aimless wandering brought her to the private library, feeling almost comforted to be surrounded by the Colonel's favourites. She still could not bring herself to open any of the finely bound volumes, no matter the promised diversions, but busied herself instead with examining the contents of his handsome writing desk.

It was the one pursuit that her presence did not distract him from. When the Colonel wrote, whether for business or pleasure, she could creep as close as she dared and he would not be brought out of his focused employment until she made a distinct noise by clearing her throat or addressing him directly.

She sat where he was wont to, envisioning his furrowed brow of concentration as the pen scratched pleasantly against paper, and the sheets filled with his bold and elegant handwriting. One of the small drawers was stuck, and it took her extra effort to dislodge it from the space it occupied. Upon its being freed, the source of its strain was evidenced by the weight of the packet of letters stacked beyond the top of the drawer, making the corner of the top letter catch against the desk.

The letters looked quite old, and were all addressed to a "Brandon" of various ranks. Marianne upbraided herself for not having considered that Colonel Brandon was once a cadet or ensign before rising to lieutenant and the following. It seemed ridiculous to think he had ever been a youth of a mere decade and some years, involved in skirmishes in the Indies, and receiving love letters from a young woman... but so he had been, and the proof was tangible in her hand.

That notorious monster known by its complexion of green took hold of Marianne, and she felt an uncontrollable jealousy towards the woman whose letters took up an entire drawer of the Colonel's writing desk, and were obviously of sentimental worth enough to preserve until now. She eagerly poured over the contents of each, momentarily confused by the author's signature as, "Mrs. Brandon." She thought the Colonel had never married. But then she recalled Mrs. Jennings offering his incomplete history which involved the coercion of Eliza Williams to marry the elder brother, and Colonel Brandon to be sent off to pursue his military career. It appeared his sister-in-law had maintained correspondence with her first love, or at least she had written him and they found their way into his possession, though it did not seem the letters had ever reached the post. Perhaps she was forced to keep the letters hidden for fear of disapproval from her own husband. Perhaps she never sent them for fear of what unhappy sentiments a returning letter might bring. Yet somehow they had come to be here in the Colonel's drawer, and Marianne was bothered by the missing pieces she wished to have in order that she might put together Colonel Brandon's and Eliza's history in full.

Frustrated with the long duration of time that had passed before she was aware of the Colonel's romance, and jealous of a poor woman who had died under the most tragic of circumstances, Marianne soon gave up her musings over the letters and quit the library, returning to her wandering about the house.

Marianne ran her hand down the length of a tassel in the yellow room, half inspecting the drapery for dust—which she knew very well was not to be found—and half stealing glances out the window it ornamented. She thought she caught a glimpse of a single rider on a black horse galloping down the drive, and in her mind could just make out the hat and cape she knew belonged to the Colonel. Before the dark shapes could get near enough for her to determine the rider's identity, she convinced herself it was indeed the Colonel returning home and fled downstairs, incurring not one, but two astonished gasps from the maids she nearly collided into on her way down.

She tried to catch her breath at the bottom of the staircase before passing into the foyer and approaching the door. She was slightly more collected, though still flushed with exertion and worry when the door was swung open by the butler, and the master stepped through.

As she went forward to greet him, eyes frantic to ascertain any injury upon him, she was paralysed with a sudden jab where her additional weight had incurred, and a definite movement that announced the presence of a growing thing from within her womb.

The Colonel stepped towards her just as she paled, gasped aloud, and clutched the place where she'd felt the babe kick. He caught her in his arms just as she passed into darkness.

When she woke again, she was not fully herself, but with head still pounding and the feeling of sickness as she had during her first weeks with child, she sank in and out of a fitful slumber.

Her dreams, when she had them, were nightmarish, echoing the terrifying thoughts of mortal combat and death that had been haunting her all morning. She tossed erratically against them, not feverish, but with symptoms akin to the same affliction. Now and then, she would call out for the Colonel, and some part of her thought he answered by soothing her forehead or clutching her hand at the worst of her terrors.

At last, she opened her eyes to the sight of Colonel Brandon at her bedside, coat discarded, and cravat undone. Exhaustion was plainly written on his features, making him appear worn and a little older than before. He looked a proper mess, but wholly intact otherwise, and oh, how Marianne loved him for it.

"Colonel Brandon," she murmured, and he stirred from his seat, concern darkening every line on his face as he took up her fragile hand in his own.

"You are not injured?" she asked, almost wishing he had rolled his sleeves back so she could see for certain that he had no lacerations or bruises.

"No," he said with some surprise. "I have sustained no injuries. Willoughby, on the other hand..." he trailed off, unable to meet her gaze for a brief moment.

"Have you killed him, then?" she asked with resignation, and the Colonel was even more surprised at how coolly she posed her question.

"I have not. I only bruised his pride and put his shooting arm out of commission for a time. I am sorry I could do no more without risking..."

"Your own life, I know," she finished for him. "I am glad you did not. And I am glad you gave him something to think on."

The Colonel grazed his thumb across the back of her hand, not having words to express what he felt, and Marianne sighed happily at the contact.

"The doctor..." Colonel Brandon began to say, clearing his throat, "The doctor was sent for, and suspects you may be with child."

Marianne smiled weakly at the notion that her pregnancy could be in question while her symptoms were so regular. "He did not confirm it, though?"

"I did not wish him to do so while you were unable to consent to a full examination."

"Ah," she said in understanding, recalling the rather uncomfortable measures taken by the poor midwife in London. "You may call for him again if you would like to have it confirmed." It was Marianne's turn to feel incapable of meeting her husband's eyes. "I am ready to acknowledge my child."

The Colonel nodded, silent again in serious thought.

"Thank you," Marianne whispered sweetly, tired from the exertion of their talk, and ready to sleep again; this time, she hoped it would be restful.

He looked at her questioningly, as if he could not make out what he was being thanked for.

"For defending my honour when I do not deserve it," she explained. "And for coming home to me safely. Thank you, Colonel."

He swallowed thickly, and smoothed some of the loosened curls away from her forehead, leaving a kiss there in his wake.

"I will send for a reputable midwife, for I am also prepared to acknowledge our child." His voice broke on the last word, and Marianne glanced up at him, wondering if she heard right, eyes filling with tears.

"The child is to take my name, is he not?" Colonel Brandon confirmed.

"Oh..." her lip quivered at the full meaning of his words. "I had not even considered... but... you mean..."

"I mean to acknowledge the child as my own, no

matter the sex."

"What of your own children?" she pressed, "What if there are more children after him? Would you not resent him after all for not being your blood?"

"The very fact that you would give me hope for future children is enough to banish all thought of possible resentment, my dear Marianne." He said her name with such tenderness and affection that the recipient of his platitudes was reduced to tears. She had thought to ask him of the letters she found in his desk, to press for confirmation that he now loved her as truly and passionately as he had his first love; to promise that she would not think it unfaithful or flighty, for she had grown to love him, and she hoped she had not kept him waiting too long.

But her heart was too heavy with the most recent confirmation of his honourable affections that she was unable to speak. She would not let him leave her, even had he wished to, but permitted him to hold her close as she cried once more and fell back to sleep in his arms.

Chapter Twelve

Not soon after Marianne's condition was announced to intimate relations—which somehow meant Mrs. Jennings was informed of the matter, and by those means, a great deal others besides—a modest dinner party was begged of the Colonel by that well-meaning, but socially prolific woman, that he and Marianne do their duty to society by introducing themselves as a married couple to all their friends and near acquaintances before his dear sweet wife was to be confined.

This suited Colonel Brandon and his "dear sweet wife," as it granted opportunity of getting several social obligations out of the way all at once, rather than putting the burden on them to make calls round about which would no doubt exhaust Marianne with excessive travel.

The dinner party was made up of those persons who might have been expected to attend the wedding had the hosting couple married in the usual way, and though the gathering had first been christened a modest one by Mrs. Jennings, the larger dining hall was filled with relations and loved ones alike by the time supper was served, and not a single spoonful of the cook's efforts to feed a grand assembly was put to waste.

Though Marianne had participated in the proceedings with the notion that this was largely to perform a societal duty, she enjoyed herself more than she expected. Great care was taken in the choosing of her gown and toilette, her mother and sisters arriving a day early to help her decide which accruements to put together, and the Colonel having made provision for whatever finery she might desire for her debut as Mrs. Brandon. A happy symptom of her condition was that her hair had a lovely lustre and fullness to it, and with the combined efforts of Elinor and the sadly lacking lady's maid, it was not too difficult to manipulate it into a thing of beauty. There were other attributes that acquired fullness, filling out her gowns nicely in the bodice which was something she had previously despaired of whenever her bouts of melancholy rendered her less than shapely in figure. It was not so now. Her complexion was of a warm and natural colour, her form was still slender besides a slight bump in her belly which was possible to conceal beneath her gowns, and all in all she was quite the picture of good health.

Mrs. Dashwood was overjoyed by Marianne's condition, excitement and nervousness rendering every action of the frantic sort, and her attempts to help quite useless to Marianne, though she was convinced everything she did was necessary and right. She fussed over her daughter standing too long, sitting too near a draft, sitting too near the sunlight, or eating enough good fruit, but more often than the rest, expressing her absolute happiness with all the unrepressed emotion her daughters expected from her.

They were able at last to redirect her energy towards a more productive avenue in assisting Elinor with the meal cards and Margaret with her dress, which was far more suitable in her own mind than to any of her family, who considered her selection rather plain and unbecoming.

Marianne found it delightful to ready herself for a dinner party without constraint on wardrobe or adornment, and being able to offer Elinor and Margaret such trim and baubles and hair combs that might suit from the bounty of her own closet. She had so often complained of the necessity of making a faded, old gown seem new with choice accessories, and it was enormously gratifying to have everything really new at her disposal and to the rescue of her sisters.

She had directed rooms to be prepared for those guests who had lengthier journeys and would therefore stay a night or two before returning to their prospective homes. Mr. John and Fanny Dashwood were of the number of those staying, and though it gave her no pleasure to prepare them a room, Marianne took care that it was done to perfection, so that even Fanny could not complain of this or that issue with housekeeping, the view, or the placement of furniture. Mrs. Pickard was made to pass on many repetitions to the footmen and maids about how this or that item was to be moved, or polished, or polished again, how the view might be enhanced by fresh paint on the window sill, or the angle of a chair moving by so many degrees. By the end of all these efforts, when it was finally deemed acceptable after the fourth or fifth scrutiny, Marianne had gained such respect from Mrs. Pickard over her determined undertaking that it was very near admiration, and she was, from that day on, quite pleased to serve her mistress and defend her decisions to the rest of the servants, which was greatly advantageous to Marianne in her position.

When the Dashwoods arrived, they made a grand show of their entrance, behaving almost as if it were Fanny herself who had acquired Colonel Brandon's estate and Marianne could not be expected to understand how things were to be managed there.

Marianne bore it astonishingly well, and the Colonel defended her admirably without suffering slight or censure to the self-important woman, though even he was tempted once or twice to offer more than an uneasy incline of the head. Marianne had not thought she could love the Colonel so well as when he accepted her illegitimate child as his own, but it appeared she was wrong once again, and Colonel Brandon consistently proved to be her defender that night in the battle of wits that was even more often in society the downfall of women.

There was one issue on which Fanny was not eager to light upon, and that was the current whereabouts of Mr. Edward Ferrars and the affianced Miss Lucy Steele. The most she would say — and that with the look of one whose teeth are being pulled — was that to call her "Miss Steele" was no longer an accurate mode of address, as she had only a day prior taken the name of Ferrars.

This announcement produced an indignant squeak from Margaret who began to say, "But I thought..." and was promptly hushed by fierce looks from both her elder sisters, and a sharp pain at her shin from her mother's kick beneath the table. The matter might have ended there, but Mrs. Jennings had all the eagerness on the subject which Fanny lacked, and well could have gone on into the night about the goodness of the two young people in question and their deserving of every happiness in the world and more besides, were it not from a loud clearing of the throat by the Colonel that arrested her attention.

"My dear Colonel! Is the bird too dry for you, or have you let it go down wrong again like that frightful day in Cleaveland—I shall never forget it!" she remarked jovially, and with a long drawn sigh as if her mother's heart went out to him. "I daresay, it is a might salty tonight, but nothing in comparison to the sad state of the partridges at Michaelmas, which we suffered through the eating of while Cook was away visiting her dying mother, poor thing. She lived a remarkable long time you know, and we were more surprised that she took as long as she did to pass on, but, really!" she exclaimed in her usual, distracted manner, putting her silver down with a clatter, "Colonel Brandon, you do seem troubled about something. Come, come, now. We are all family here; you must not keep secrets. You know how gifted Sir Middleton and I are at wheedling things out of you! Out with it, sir, and do not make yourself a solitary martyr without cause."

"Why should I be troubled with such a lovely

wife and good friends about me?" the Colonel countered, his features softening as a smile played about the corners of his mouth.

"That is just as I would expect you to answer, you naughty man, and in so doing you have not given us a real answer at all," Mrs. Jennings complained, but she let the matter drop nonetheless as Elinor had tactfully broached her with questions of how Charlotte and her newborn son were.

The Colonel and Marianne exchanged looks over the near disaster of conversation; he with harried concern for her sister, and she with tender gratitude that he would be so openly troubled by a subject that might cause Elinor pain. The remainder of the evening passed by pleasantly, and with no more terrible frights by the mention of Edward's or Lucy's name, nor so much as a reference to a similar situation which might arouse interest in them. This was largely due to the unspoken agreement between the Brandons and the Dashwoods to do everything in their power to keep the rest of the company entertained and sufficiently distracted by any means to prevent the matter arising again. Such an alliance was astonishing, indeed, and was a strange business to have Elinor's feeling and Fanny's pride so tangled up in the same disappointing man.

Marianne was quick to thank the Colonel when they were alone again. She had been so concerned over her sister during the course of the evening that she could not even be bothered to find insult in the request from Fanny to be sent up a servant to rearrange the room she'd been given.

"Thank you for looking after Elinor," she remarked whilst tying the ribbon round the end of her braid. "She might not easily show how affected she is by Edward's marriage, but I know she must be heartbroken." Her hands dropped to her side and she expelled a sigh. "I did not think they would marry so soon! Ah, but... I had almost forgotten..." she shifted in her chair to address the Colonel directly, "They are to live here. Within walking distance, even. I suppose your offer was a great deal more than acceptable to them both," she said, and hoped it was not too bitterly uttered. She stood and began to tighten the ribbons on her robe, a thing somewhat strange if she intended on retiring to bed soon.

"Did you not read my letter to Mr. Ferrars?" the Colonel queried, "I had given you leave to."

"Yes, I know, but I was much too struck by the contents of the letter addressed to *me* that I was unable to bring myself to look at the other." She said nothing of the collection of romantic correspondences she'd discovered in the little drawer that day of the duel, but decided to hold her peace until a more appropriate time. "I trust you were as kind and noble as I know you to be," she said with a toss of her head in his direction, and he could not tell if she was in earnest or not.

"I am honoured that you place such blind faith in me," he said with caution, "but I had wished you to read it, if only to tell me if I had overstepped my place in what I'd said regarding your sister."

"What do you mean?!" Marianne started, becoming instantly agitated. "You mentioned Elinor! I did not know..! Oh, I wish I had read it, now! But whatever did you say?"

"It seems to have made no difference in his decision to marry Miss Steele, though he has not written me to accept the living, which thing I find strange. Unless some other, more appealing means of vocation has been presented to them."

"That is not likely," Marianne dismissed the thought at once. "But, Colonel! Will you not tell me what you said?"

He rather enjoyed having her enthralled by his revelation, and the expectation of what was to still be revealed. It made him hesitant to inform too quickly. He wished to linger a little longer with those wondering eyes fixated entirely upon him, as if he were the only one that mattered in that moment. "I only told him the terms of the living, and how suitable we found the cottage—that the plot was serviceable for keeping chickens and grazing cattle. As your sister was a great influence in these matters, it is only natural that her efforts were acknowledged. I'm certain he knew of whom I referred. He could not mistake it, I think."

"Then you never so much as mentioned Elinor by name?" she frowned, disappointed after all.

"I did not. Although I did say there was a young lady, a very close relation to my wife who was staying with us, and seemed quite determined to make the cottage pleasing for his sake. I said that duty was admirable, but it was a pity that duty and heart could not always be reconciled."

"Oh, Colonel!" she cried, and surprised him by bounding towards him with an expression of utter happiness. He held her by her arms, afraid she might injure herself by colliding with him in her eagerness. "I am so glad that you said so! Ah..." she quickly became downcast, "But he has married Lucy anyway. I do not understand him!"

Colonel Brandon was having a remarkably difficult time understanding his wife's dizzying change in emotions, and was battling his own temptation at having her pressed so close to his body while she looked up at him, flushed and excited. "He... is not his own man, my... Marianne, but bound by duty to keep his word."

A look then was given him by his wife, one that clearly stated her feeling on *that* subject, and the poor excuse she thought it.

Colonel Brandon loosened his hold on her, feeling uncomfortable under such a gaze, though he would not completely relinquish his possession, and asked if she was angry with him.

It was then she finally gained awareness of their interesting position. Marianne coloured as the warmth rose to her cheeks, and the Colonel felt her arms stiffen beneath the favourite robe she wore. She swallowed and coughed a little in embarrassment. "No, Colonel. I believe you have done everything one could have asked of you in such circumstances, and more besides."

His breath and all memory of how to reclaim it abandoned him in the instant Marianne reached up and placed a sweet, short kiss upon his lips. He let her go in his astonishment. One hand nearly brushed the small of her back while the other hovered very close to her cheek, but he did not dare to bring himself to touch her.

"Oh, Marianne..." he sounded sad, she thought; perhaps even on the verge of tears. She waited, nervously anticipating his rejection of her; his regretful sentiments and the dismissal of previous feelings that no longer swayed him.

"Do you intend on sleeping soon?" Whether the question was full of implications for activities most often conducted within a bed, or merely a form of distraction so that he might find a way out of his current situation, she could not tell.

"I do," she murmured softly, searching his eyes, and aching to know whether she had made some dreadful mistake and wishing desperately he would give some indication of what he was thinking, "but I think Elinor must be very low tonight."

She hated to ask in such a moment, but as Colonel Brandon was not reciprocating her forward action, and the lack of clarity was making her anxious to flee, she asked, "May I go to her?"

"Whatever you wish," he said, and Marianne felt it a little too brusque. At her hesitance, he said more patiently, "Of course, if Elinor would be comforted by your presence, you should be with her tonight."

"You will not take this as a rejection?" she asked, almost fearfully.

"Only if you insist upon it being one." He smiled without real joy, and Marianne hated to be torn between her sister's crisis and her own.

"Here is my answer," she said, reaching up to try another kiss.

He was slightly more prepared for her this time, and dared to catch her lips as they were raised to him, making them linger for the briefest moment longer than before. After what seemed an eternity, and yet far, far too soon, he let her go. As she slipped from his arms and out the door, she turned back once to look at him with cheeks aglow and eyes alight; burning with some new sentiment he did not recognise in her. Colonel Brandon sighed at her departure and thought it a pity indeed that she was not to share his bed that evening.

Chapter Thirteen

Life at Barton Cottage remained much the same as it always had for Elinor, at least to all outward appearances. She helped Betsy and her mother; pressed drapes, mended clothing, dusted furniture, and baked bread, and was as much an industrious woman transplanted to the countryside as she ever had been upon first inhabiting the cottage with her mother and two sisters. The greatest difference lay, of course, in Marianne's absence, which was an alteration felt by all. The house was a great deal quieter, for one. Mama was still as verbally forceful and decidedly open about her opinions, but did not retain the same measure of continuity without Marianne to encourage and exacerbate her. Though Elinor missed her sister's lively company, she could not pretend to be wholly displeased with the hush of silence that overtook the little house more often than not; when Margaret was outside and her mother in the garden, and even sometimes when they were all together in the house and no one had much to say in the way of tumultuous sentiments.

Her mother felt Marianne's absence most—

though she was by no means unhappy to think of her dearest child in that grand house only eight miles away — and Margaret, too, felt the loss more than if Elinor had gone, she was certain of that. Elinor's serious disposition and unwavering determination to fulfil one's moral duty did not suit such a young and impetuous girl. Margaret was not romantic in the same way that Marianne was, but neither was she happy to sit for an hour or more at a time in order to learn French grammar or improve her copybook; her thirst for imaginary adventures proved impossible to slate by focused and regulated study.

The gap in age was not so very great between Elinor and Margaret, but with a sister between them the gap seemed greater, and Elinor understood the inevitable bond that Marianne and Margaret would share, considering similarities in disposition and a shared enthusiasm for all things amiable to youthful sensibilities. However, with Marianne away, and no diversions more readily accessible than one another's company, Elinor and Margaret grew to understand each other better by and by, and Margaret even accepted some of Elinor's influence with more sincerity than Marianne had at the same age.

There was one haunting thought which cast a dark cloud over the pleasant steadiness of Elinor's everyday life, and that was the knowledge that any day would bring Edward and his new wife to Delaford where they would establish themselves permanently at the Rectory. She wondered that she had not yet received a letter from Marianne, telling her that they'd come and to be on the lookout. She did not think it likely that she would fail to mention such a significant event, since Marianne knew how anxious Elinor would be to prepare herself for any possible chance of their meeting, whether in consideration of her next visit to Delaford, or by accidental meeting in a gathering of friends hosted by Mrs. Jennings that might not be politely avoided. It had been days since the dinner party in which their marriage had been made known, and Elinor had heard nothing of Edward's whereabouts nor of his official acceptance of the position there.

Elinor sprinkled more flour over the lump of dough she turned over on the shelf, and worked the soft powder in with her knuckles. The methodical work gave her something to focus on besides the lack of communication from Marianne. Until that moment, Margaret had been watching in disinterested silence, but now she interrupted Elinor's unspoken thoughts with a question of geography.

"What are the five rivers of Punjab that flow into the Indus?"

"I do not know," Elinor admitted. "You had better consult your atlas rather than me, dear."

A peculiar lethargy had overtaken Margaret that afternoon and she idled with a cheesecloth rather than heeding any mind to Elinor's suggestion. "Colonel Brandon would know without looking at the atlas," she complained.

"I daresay he would, but the Colonel has been to the East Indies and would have an easier time remembering the names of rivers he might have had reason to come across during his military exploits."

"Do you think he misses travelling in such exotic, faraway places?" Margaret asked wistfully. "If I should go to India, I don't know that I would ever want to return."

"Perhaps," she mused, "Although he was there as a soldier, under circumstances that were not always pleasant, so I believe it more than reasonable to assume he is far happier now, having settled back in England."

"Do you mean by marrying Marianne, or taking possession of Delaford?" she put slyly, and with more understanding than her sisters were likely to give her credit for.

"I mean both, dearest. I am confident he is even happier now than when he first became master of Delaford."

"How could you know such a thing for certain?" Margaret questioned dubiously.

"It is not difficult to tell. Especially when one does more observing than interrogating," she said with a meaningful raise of her brows, and a playful smile.

Margaret grumbled to have been so easily defeated, but soon brightened at the thought of something else to test her eldest sister by, clearly undeterred by the jab at her methods of questioning. "Would you have liked to marry someone with a grand estate, Elinor? With two libraries, and two dining halls, and more rooms than a whole dinner party can fill at night?" Their recent stay at Delaford was still fresh in her mind, and the experience had left a curious impression on her. "Do you find it hard not to be jealous of

Marianne?"

"I think not," Elinor said with perfect candour and a small smile hidden by her head lowered over her task. "I would not reject a man for having a grand estate and wealth besides, but they are not inducements to jealousy for me. I am grown very used to the busy methods of a modest living, and I know now that I prefer it to a life of luxury and idleness."

The idea of two libraries suddenly did not hold as much allurement for Margaret at the mention of idleness. "Is Marianne very bored at the great house?"

Elinor laughed softly. "Not dangerously so," she said, taking care not to be dishonest with her sister. "Not at present, that is, and being with child she is allowed some measure of idleness."

"But you should not like to always be dressed handsomely and hosting dinner parties to fashionable people like John and Fanny, should you, Elinor?"

"No. Would you?" she asked with real interest, pausing in her kneading to await Margaret's answer.

Margaret tossed her head with an emphatic, "No. But then..." she amended, thinking it over more carefully, "If *I* had a rich husband with a large estate, I could always find some form of excitement in riding horses, or travelling expeditions sponsored by my husband's wealth, or even by inviting all sorts of interesting people to my home. Perhaps I could host parties, but for foreign diplomats or privateers seeking asylum."

"I think that a suitable compromise to being

idle. All but for the last part," she cautioned laughingly.

Margaret giggled, but refrained from argument, considering the conversation at an end.

Elinor sighed as she continued working the bread, sadly trying and yet failing terrifically to imagine Lucy Steele—now Ferrars—tending to all the necessities of the parsonage and Edward's parishioners. She would need to minister to those of both high and low estate, showing partiality to none. She would be required to ensure that the household and the manner of their lifestyle could be supported by Edward's modest salary. She must take care that the curtains she chose for the sitting room were not too heavy for the thin rod that would bear them up. The requirements Elinor conceived for Edward's wife to possess were impossible standards for many a better woman than even Lucy to strive for, and the thought made Elinor more unhappy than she cared to admit.

Margaret had grown tired of watching her sister prepare the evening meal, and had been easing her way towards the hall and the open door for some time. She now let out an excited squeal, announcing that there was a rider on his way to them this very moment. She bounded away to find her mother, and shouted throughout the house, "It is Edward! Mama, I think Edward has come!"

She returned to her sister, but seeming to recollect Edward's recent marriage, her countenance fell in devastation and sympathy. "E... Elinor," she stuttered, "It's... Edward is come."

Elinor tried in vain to appear untouched by this unexpected arrival. She hastily wiped the flour on her apron, and made her way to the sitting room where Mrs. Dashwood had been transported by Margaret's enthusiastic cries. She inspected her eldest daughter with a terrific gleam in her eye that conveyed part horror, part pity. She bade Elinor turn around, and released her from the floured apron with as much speed as her trembling fingers were capable of.

When Edward entered, it might have appeared to him as if they had all three been quietly sitting for hours. They rose to receive him with all due formality, and the subsequent silence that immediately befell them lasted just long enough to be uncomfortable. Nobly desirous of re-establishing an easy repertoire with their good friend of old, Mrs. Dashwood reached forward, and taking his hands in her own, said, "Dear Edward! We wish you joy."

"I... I thank you," he said as if her thoughtfulness took him by surprise. Elinor wondered if the recent cruelty of his relations caused him astonishment to find friendship elsewhere. It pained her for his sake to think it could be so.

Mrs. Dashwood offered Edward a chair, and he took it, though rather stiffly. That awful silence once more filled the room, and Margaret took the lead by remarking on the fine weather they had been enjoying. Edward smiled, looking moderately more at ease, and agreed that the roads were very dry.

"Are you... settled, then, at the parsonage?" Mrs. Dashwood continued, grasping for a topic to increase discussion by. Elinor had still not found the courage to speak.

"I am on my way now. I thought to impose on your good will by stopping here, first, as I... had something... Barton Cottage has always been dear to me." He could not bear meeting Mrs. Dashwood's searching look, and though she inwardly recoiled from furthering the topic of his marriage, she could contrive of no other way to have the uncomfortable wedge between them done away with.

"Have you left Mrs. Ferrars in London?"

"No," he blinked confusedly. "No, my mother is returned to Norland Park. I thought you would have seen her at Delaford recently."

"I did not inquire after your mother, but your wife," she amended softly. "Mrs. Edward Ferrars."

Edward started in his seat, turning his head slightly in Elinor's direction and quickly back to Mrs. Dashwood. "Then... you have not heard? I had thought... I wrote to the Colonel, explaining my change in circumstance. Lucy has married Robert. She is Mrs. Robert Ferrars, now."

Elinor let out a cross between a choke and a whimper, the first display of thought or emotion since the beginning of their conversation.

Edward stood, not knowing where to let his gaze fall, and found himself nervously playing with the ears of a porcelain lamb upon the mantle as he explained. "Lucy wrote to me, confessing a transfer of affection to my brother. They were much together in London, it seems, and bearing in mind my recently... changed circumstances, I only thought it right to, um, release her from the engagement."

"Then," Elinor begged, her voice strained with her attempt at self-composure as she stood to ascertain whether or not this strange dream was able to persevere, "You are not... married?"

Edward answered her statement with a nod of affirmation, hope evident in his eyes.

No longer able to contain the feelings that afflicted her, having gone from hopeless resignation to despondent indignation, and back to resolute despair all within the course of the past hour, and now to be suddenly struck with such a real and tangible hope before her, it was all too much. She let out a cry, falling back hard into the chair, and releasing the veritable storm of emotions from the weeks and months she had suffered a broken heart in silence.

At this uncharacteristic outburst, Mrs. Dashwood hastened from the room, dragging Margaret with her, and making no pretence of subtlety as she did so. Margaret followed as far as her mother's bedroom door, and then petitioned that she might run outside to sit in the tree house rather than join her mama in her relentless pacing across the room. Mrs. Dashwood assented distractedly and Margaret ran back downstairs, stopping just before the entrance of the sitting room in order to shamelessly eavesdrop, something Marianne in the long run was most grateful for.

Elinor was sitting too near the doorway for Margaret to see her, but she *heard* her, as she was vainly struggling to suppress her crying.

Edward was in the midst of explanation, it seemed, for his previous engagement and behaviour.

"Elinor, I met Lucy when I was very young — we both were very young. Had I an active profession then, I never would have had such a foolish inclination. My behaviour at Norland was very wrong. I could not imagine you would care for me as I did you, and I convinced myself it was my heart alone that I risked. I have come here today, not with any expectation, but only to tell you, now I am at liberty to do so, that my heart is and always will be... yours."

Margaret stole a glance into the room, and Edward was bringing himself to one knee. Feeling a sudden and unexpected guilt for spying, she left her post just as he was taking Elinor's hand in his, but what the end of their exchange was, even young Margaret did not have difficulty imagining.

Chapter Fourteen

The startling revelation that Lucy Ferrars had *not* married Edward had been brought to Delaford even before Edward had come to Elinor, in the most ordinary of ways, and that through the post. One might have expected the original informant to be Mrs. Jennings, who certainly would pass on the news the very moment she heard a word of it spoken, and make everyone even remotely affected aware of the shocking revelation with exceeding haste, but the source of the information came direct by Edward's own hand, in a letter to Colonel Brandon.

The missive in which Mr. Edward Ferrars broke the news of his altered situation was more a profession of gratitude than anything else. His exaltations of Colonel Brandon's generosity were extensive indeed, and his words bore an impression that he considered his good fortune due solely to the influence of the Colonel's sister-in-law, Miss Dashwood, for he could not imagine why someone with whom he shared no other connection would provide him a living.

The letter held a great deal more to offer in the matter of inheritance and income; things not at all interesting to the feminine sensibilities of Mrs. Brandon, whom the Colonel kept in mind when he brought his wife the letter and directed her to read which pages would prove most significant to her. He was correct to assume that the monetary details were of little consequence to her; she skimmed whole paragraphs that did not deal directly with Edward's marital status and consequential intentions in moving to Delaford's rectory. There was much to sift through regarding self-disparagement and unworthiness — more, certainly than even the Colonel thought entirely sensible, and though Marianne agreed with Edward's confessed faults, she did not particularly relish the reading of them — but at length, she reached the portion of the letter that contained every detail of his broken engagement, Lucy's change of heart, his brother's acquisition of her affections and hand in marriage, and the subsequent hope it rekindled in her for Elinor's sake.

Edward admitted humbly that despite his lack of wife, he was still in need of a vocation and living, and if the Colonel was of such a generous mind to allow him Delaford's parish, he would happily accept, and forever be indebted to him. He wrote as one already indebted to the Colonel for the very act of writing him, and he was certain Colonel Brandon could not know the full measure of relief and hope he'd felt in being recipient to such a correspondence. Elinor's name was never mentioned, her person never directly made reference to, but Marianne thought she was not too presumptuous to infer from Edward's letter that it was now for her sister he thought and planned.

To both Marianne and the Colonel, the question now remained as to what all should be told to Elinor. Of course they agreed that she should know Edward would be coming to Delaford, and soon, but in what manner and in what detail to alert her were the decisions they could not seem to agree upon.

Both were almost certain by the tone of the letter that Edward meant to offer himself to Elinor, though the Colonel reserved more apprehension in the light of how recently things had been settled between him and Lucy. Marianne, however, said she would be very much surprised, and ashamed of him as well, if Edward did not immediately saddle a horse and ride unceasingly day and night to make his proposal, now that he was free to do so. She said that if he truly loved her sister, there should be nothing he would endure by way of obstacle to securing her happiness and heart—now that the securing of both was nearly in reach—and they should tell Elinor at once so that she might prepare for his arrival.

Colonel Brandon was wary of raising Elinor's expectations on the chance Edward proved slack in his pursuit of her. It was Edward's role and responsibility to inform his lady, if indeed she was his, that his hand and heart were free to offer to whom he would.

In the end, he was persuaded with the knowledge that Marianne knew her sister better than he, and if she considered it best to convey the full circumstances of Edward Ferrars's arrival, he would abide by her wishes and allow her the honour of writing to her at once. Marianne would have liked to go to Elinor and speak to her in person, but she had been experiencing more pains of late and did not feel up to the journey, short as it was. So a letter was eventually decided on. Marianne intended to keep it as brief and succinct as possible for one carrying such weighty news, but she found she had so much to tell of her own strong feelings on the matter, and the many nothings that befell her over the days since Elinor's removal from Delaford and the last dinner party, that by the end of it, Edward's broken engagement and the likeliness of his being in the county made up less than a third of the letter, and its journey through the post was unintentionally delayed due to its contents taking more than one sitting to conclude.

Before the letter had reached Elinor, Edward himself had arrived in Dorsetshire, stopping first at Barton, under the accurate assumption that he would always be welcome at the cottage. It was therefore the haste of his journeying, and the accidental delay of Marianne's correspondence that had Edward calling upon Mrs. Dashwood and her two remaining daughters at home before Elinor had been made to know the nature of his visit to that part of the country.

Margaret proved herself a worthy informant for Marianne, as she wrote to her in novelesque elaboration the entirety of Edward's visit, including the suitability of his modest situation to Elinor's desire to remain industrious, as she had confessed to Margaret only minutes before accepting

Edward's proposal.

As the parish was already prepared for new residents, there was no reason to delay the publishing of their banns, and both Edward and Elinor were determined that their engagement should last no longer than was strictly necessary for the sake of propriety. There was an unspoken understanding amongst those dear to them why a long engagement was not to be tolerated, and Colonel Brandon was as much admired for his provision that allowed them a short engagement as any might expect.

Marianne refused to begin her confinement until after the wedding, though she made no promises of doing so immediately following, either. It was a point of amiable contention between her and the Colonel, who though wary of the doctor's insistence of a prolonged lie-in, did not believe Marianne always the best judge of her own abilities and health. She assured him most emphatically that she would rest as soon as she felt it necessary, but had done so much lying-in already due to melancholy and discontent that she wished to be at least a little active and useful to her sister for as long as she might.

Edward and Elinor were married on a Sunday morning after services, in the very chapel which sacred duties Edward would be bound to from now on. The church was adorned with wildflowers and garlands which the parishioners had seen fit to place about the church only hours before. Elinor had a new gown of printed muslin in a lovely blue, being persuaded by her mother and sisters to purchase materials less sturdy and practical than she might have without their influence, but by no means was tempted into a finer muslin, nor would she have anything to do with silks. Marianne supposed it was best that her gown not be too garish for a minister's wife, but had insisted on lending her gloves at least, and gifted her a bonnet which she thought suited Elinor better.

Margaret was looking more on the side of fourteen than her nearly-thirteen years, and particularly pretty in one of Marianne's old frocks Mama had spruced up for the occasion. She had taken special care with the arrangement of her hair, and was even more interested in listening attentively to the ceremony and wishing Edward and Elinor happiness than tossing the petals after them with the congregants as she might have once before.

Marianne could not help but wonder if Margaret's new found gentility had anything to do with the tall young lad sitting eagerly to attention in the second-to-front pew of the assembly. She did seem most pleased to introduce his aunt and cousins with whom he lived to Marianne and the Colonel as soon as the gathering of well-wishers had filtered out enough to make room for proper introductions. Though it would be two years still before she was out and able to receive offers of courtship, Marianne knew well that youth cared little for society's standards of appropriate feeling, and she determined to pay as much heed as possible to any of Margaret's favourite persons, whether serious attachments or not.

The ride home in the carriage was filled with the pleasant recollection of all that Marianne had found excellent and endearing, no matter that they had just come from the church, or that the Colonel was there to see it all for himself; she relished in the reliving of it all, and he had no objections to the ramblings of her cheerfulness.

"But I have gone on long enough without pause," she remarked after a time, "What are your thoughts on the new couple, Colonel? Do you think they will be happy, despite the tiny pasture for their flock, and the weak curtain rods that will barely support the drapes, and the smoky furnace?" she said in mirth.

"I think it impossible for them to be otherwise, with such mutual affection to secure their future," he answered more seriously. "Edward Ferrars is a fortunate man, indeed."

"I cannot pretend to mistake your meaning," she replied, her voice turning soft and low. "I... I have a confession to make, and... I fear I've put it off for too long already." Marianne twisted her gloves in her lap, nervously anticipating her confession. She intended to declare her love to him at that very moment as the carriage—which she considered superfluous for such a short distance, but he insisted upon it—rolled gently across the scenic grounds of Delaford. The driver had been commanded to go slowly so that their passage might be all the more smooth, and Marianne could not complain, for it allowed her to consider a while before uttering such a momentous revelation too hastily.

Colonel Brandon frowned in curiosity. "Does something trouble you?"

"Yes, I can't *bear* keeping secrets," she expressed

with more force than she meant to convey, "for it's as close to lying most will allow themselves while maintaining their sphere of moral uprightness, and many people *do* keep secrets with little thought as to how great a gulf it can create before it divides them completely. I am not saying our secrets will divide us, for we're not... we have not begun our marriage so very like most are begun."

"Do you mean that I keep something from you, or you from me?" he wondered aloud.

"I found the letters from Eliza." She couldn't say what prompted those words to come spilling out of her mouth, as they were nothing like the ones she'd meant to speak. "On the day you fought Willoughby. I was lonely, and I searched your writing desk to find them there. Oh!" she interjected, "That sounds terribly nosy, but I was not snooping on purpose, Colonel, I promise! I was only curious, and there are so many of them tied prettily with ribbon..." she trailed off, no longer certain of how to finish her thought.

"My brother gave them to me upon her death," he explained simply.

"Ah. Then you were not... in correspondence with her while in the Indies?"

"No," he frowned. "And I was not the cause for their divorce, either."

"Did you... were you in love with her all that while?"

He sighed, and she was almost sorry for asking, as his features darkened considerably. "I was. I am... thankful, in a way that the letters were not able to reach me until she had passed. I might have done something very foolish had I known she regretted me too."

Marianne had a fleeting moment in which she considered saying no more, but she was truly interested in her husband's past, and decided that if he was unwilling to speak of it he would tell her so. "What would you have done?" she questioned.

"Perhaps if I was at liberty, I would have caused their divorce as well as coerced Eliza to elopement. Perhaps we would have done worse, and not risked a break with the family by secretly carrying on behind their back—behind my brother's back. Our love was... ungrounded in any true merit. It was hasty, and impetuous, and foolhardy. I was warned of her darker propensities that had not even materialised fully at that time, but I was too blinded by infatuation to see any of her faults. When she put Beth in my care, I could tell she had not been driven to her waywardness merely by my brother's unloving ways, but her own unsettled soul as well."

Marianne's next question was posed with an even softer voice than her last, and her eyes remained fixated on the fidgeting of her hands as she asked, "Do you love her still?"

"I do not," he broke gently. "I am sometimes regretful that we could not have been what we were once before, though I am long since disillusioned of that possibility. But I know your views on first love and how it is never to be replaced or renewed." His tone transitioned to one of a slow, methodical kind. He spoke as he did when there was something grave he had to relate and expected Marianne's swift and open disapproval. "I know that you must think me unfaithful to the memory of my youthful love, but I cannot repent of my newer affections. I *choose* not to repent. If loving you with a greater depth and sorrow of the heart than I have ever loved Eliza, or could ever love her is a sin in your eyes, then it is a sin I must take to my grave, for I have no apology, nor will I be dishonest enough to pretend one."

Marianne was crying quietly, but as she made no sighs or sobs, he did not realise it until he looked to her for a reply, and was met with a downcast head and her fruitless attempts to staunch the trace of tears before the next onslaught of them trailed down her mottled cheeks.

"Do not distress yourself, Mrs. Brandon. I beg you would not," he moved forward as if considering whether or not to take the seat beside her. "I am well aware of your feelings towards me and harbour no frustrations against you. I could hardly expect you to love a man so above you in age and below you in beauty. I will not misinterpret the kiss you bestowed upon me a week ago as anything more than a method of thanks in a giddy moment. I am only thankful that such a precious gift was granted me, and I will ask no more—I shall expect nothing else, but simply learn to content myself as the kindly old man who on rare occasion might have the ability to make you smile." He tried to smile himself, but failed to make the expression reach his eyes.

Marianne was so struck by his speech that her tears had only increased rather than abated for the duration of it. They had arrived at the gate of their home before she could collect herself enough for a proper reply, but when he offered his hand to help her step down from the carriage, she grasped his forearm and clung to it tightly, not willing to loosen her grip until they were safely alone in the corridor which she drew him into as soon as the servants had divested them of hat, gloves, and outer coats.

Her hands trembled, even as she deliberately pulled him away to speak her mind. Colonel Brandon worried over her pained expression and tear-stricken face. "Are you unwell? Have I distressed you?" He attempted to usher her into the nearest room, "Come and sit in the parlour and I will have something brought for you to drink."

"Colonel Brandon, please stay a moment," she begged, resisting his intentions of moving her from the corridor. "I *must* speak with you. I was not finished confessing to you in the carriage, and if I am not allowed to say what I meant to, I may never find the courage again."

"Courage?" he echoed, and she nodded rather piteously.

"Yes, the courage to let go of my stubborn pride, and admit that I was wrong," she explained in sincerity. "I no longer believe that there cannot be love after loss, or that it is unfaithful to accept the truth of past indiscretions or misplaced affection. My heart has changed so much these few months, and I am learning that love may prove itself in ways more precious and steadfast through quiet perseverance than all the violent platitudes of unreserved passion. My change of heart is all due to you, Colonel Brandon, and your patience with me. I..." she faltered but briefly, fluttering her eyes upwards in order to declare, "I do not see you as a kindly old man, devoid of appeal or riddled with infirmities. Those were foolish misjudgements I made before I knew you, and certainly before we were wed. I think you the best of husbands," she reached to cup his cheek with the softest of touches, and he leaned into her palm, fearing to release the breath he'd inhaled lest the spell of her touch be broken, "I think you the dearest of men, and I love you as such. As a wife ought to love her husband. That is what I wished for you to know. That is the secret I have kept for too long."

Tears were now making silent treks down the Colonel's weathered face, and he shuddered with emotion as Marianne traced them away with her thumb. "Marianne," he warned hoarsely, foregoing any formality of speech, "I might kiss you, now."

"I might be very scandalous and allow it," she whispered, her darkened eyes and eager expression indicating that she not only allowed, but desired it.

"And what if the servants come upon us?" he questioned, bringing to mind their position in the corridor, which was not as private a location as might be wholly appropriate for a display of spousal affection. Yet even as he asked, his hand snaked around her waist to draw her closer until the small, round bump at her belly was flush against his own body, proving he was not at all concerned for the servants' sake.

Marianne now trembled with emotions of a very different nature than before. "You mean to ask; what if the servants spy a husband and wife behaving in a romantic fashion? I suppose they will infer that I am in love with you, and you with me," she smiled enticingly.

"Then their inference would be correct," was his gruff response, and he mirrored her gesture by holding her cheek with his free hand and claiming her lips with his own.

Chapter Fifteen

On the night of Marianne's confession, she and Colonel Brandon shared a bed. It was not in the manner of couples consummating a marriage, for even though Marianne had made it known that such intercourse would be welcome, the Colonel was most careful for her and the growing child in every way imaginable. It took her an excessive amount of reassurances to even bring him to hold her to him as they slept, and she was not persuaded that he slept very comfortably after all, for he was stiff and slow to movement the following morning.

It was not, perhaps, the most romantic of ways to awaken; urgent for the chamber pot, with a husband groaning over his sore joints and then pretending he had done so such thing, but there was a strange charm to their complaints in that it felt quite the usual thing for a married couple to do, and it was the first time since her wedding Marianne felt truly married. For while they were not engaging in such intimate acts that bawdy novels proclaimed essential, and even better authorities accepted as necessary for making two as one, still they were comfortable with one another's morning practices; a world in which only the most intimate of relations and trusted of servants were permitted.

Despite her romanticising the simple voicing of bodily needs, Marianne took issue with the Colonel's constant fear of her causing herself or the babe injury, and told him so as they took their tea in her boudoir. He seemed incapable of allowing her so much as to prepare the tea, but bade her let the servant see to it while she sat and waited for it to be brought to her. It was not such an unpleasant situation altogether, but it reminded her of the thousand other little things she might not wish to be protected from quite so religiously.

"Colonel," she said, once the servant had gone, and they had exchanged morning greetings befitting a tea service, "I am not so delicate a creature that I will break by one wrong touch or movement. As unkind as my presumptions upon your person being decrepit in its agedness was, you must see how your treating me as fragile is also unpleasant."

He frowned in disagreement whilst passing her a fully doctored cup of tea—her second already. "It was not until I held you that I realised how... truly with child you are."

Marianne laughed, embarrassing the Colonel. "I could not be more or less with child! I either am or I am not!"

"I... cannot know how to elaborate on my meaning without giving insult," he sniffed, hiding his discomfort with a prolonged sip of tea.

"You meant that I have become quite *round*, and you did not notice until you tried to wrap your arms around my girth? But Colonel, you have never held me before to have a comparison!"

His expression indicated that it was not a fact he particularly cared to have verbalised. "I confess it is strange to share a bed, and to be close to you, and to touch you where I know the child lives and grows."

Marianne paused, trying to appreciate the peculiarity of his situation. "The woman in London who confirmed my condition told me a great many things I had not known before, regarding conception and childbirth. At the time I thought it much more than I should ever hope to know, but now I almost wish I'd been more curious, and asked her my own questions."

Without being too pronounced in her implications, Marianne went on soberly, surprising herself by her composure. "She claimed there was no danger to either me or the baby to engage in intercourse, and I thought it cold comfort at the time as I never imagined I'd be using it as argument against my husband. *For* my husband," she amended, smilingly.

The sideways glance he afforded her was brief, but full of meaning. "It is not only your safety, and that of the child's that I am anxious for. I do not wish to disturb you. You sleep so sweetly, and I am afraid of waking you by turning too often."

"You forget that I shared a bed with my sister for most of my life," Marianne reminded him. "Besides cold feet there is little that disturbs my sleep once I have begun it."

"Much like your love, your sleep is constant, is that what you mean to tell me?"

"You are quite poetic this morning, Colonel."

"I have a wife who is teaching me well." So saying, he abandoned his drained teacup for a much sweeter pursuit of kissing his rosy-cheeked wife.

It was not many days before Marianne changed her tune, and the amorous ideas that were so encouraged by her one morning over tea were suddenly abhorrent to the extreme. She still would not hear of lying-in, but took her walks in every kind of weather, except those expressly forbidden by the Colonel, and as he usually accompanied her, there was little she could do against his wishes.

Food became a challenge rather than a joy, as something that would tempt her one day might have a nauseating affect the very next. Marianne wondered how she would ever have borne her condition in a marriage without wealth, as she was certain her fickle palate was not conducive to economical living.

She confessed as much to Elinor, who smiled in her knowing way and said it was fortunate, then, that Marianne would never have to know the necessities of economising. Marianne then realised that Elinor would have to bear all of her pregnancies without the constant aid of monetary provisions, and she blushed and tried to rescind her remark. But Elinor was not offended in the least, and had every confidence that when her own time came, she would manage contentedly, just as she had always managed.

Edward and Elinor were as industrious as she

could have hoped and a great deal more besides. Amongst her home improvements, their ministering to the parishioners day and night—for neither of them could close their ears to the needs of those less fortunate, no matter the hour—and the care and feeding of their livestock, Elinor had little time for making social calls, though she visited the great house as often as she could. Marianne began to feel with some resentment that they lived in two separate worlds. She still longed for her sister's presence, her confidence, and her company, but life amongst grand rooms with a host of servants at her disposal called for concerns of a very different nature from Elinor's. It was not as if the two sisters could not sympathise with each other, or struggle to comprehend the problems of the other, but their daily duties and preferred recreations were so removed from one another that Marianne sometimes found herself thinking wistfully of their girlhood, and regretting she had not taken better care of their friendship before adulthood and married life had inevitably estranged them in certain aspects of their lives.

Their one constancy was the Sabbath, when all the villagers gathered at the chapel, and after Edward's sermon, he and his wife took lunch at the great house. The four people so dear to each other spent the whole of the afternoon in the best of company, until they gathered with the parishioners again for Evensong, and then at last to part ways.

Marianne thought marriage made vast improvements to Edward's character. When his natural shyness was overcome, his behaviour gave every indication of an open and affectionate heart.

At ease with his wife, he was far less inclined to ramble sardonically, or give opinions Marianne found of ghastly poor taste. Their disagreements were far less of an incredulous, baiting nature, and more amiable discussion. Yet, her marriage to Colonel Brandon had also tempered Marianne, and she was far less inclined to find fault with people in general, least of all her brother-in-law who clearly made her sister so very happy.

It was one Sunday afternoon, a very fine day in late spring, while Elinor and Marianne took a turn about the grounds—not too far, as Elinor was aware that prolonged wandering by Marianne made the Colonel nervous—as they passed the hedgerow and out of sight of the windows, that a particular person of worthy note, though not of worthy character, came upon them suddenly, causing Marianne to stumble back in fear and surprise.

As the imposing figure drew nearer, he pushed his hat over his brow so as to obscure his identity from any who might be watching from afar, though there was no mistaking whose dark riding coat cloaked his shoulders, nor whose horse he now walked by the bridle.

Though startled to see him come upon them so suddenly, Marianne had regained her composure in an instant, only holding a little tighter to Elinor's arm, hoping it was not a visible shift in her posture. She had sometimes thought of what she might say to him if such a circumstance presented itself, as impossible as it seemed, and now that he stood before her with at least the good sense to look something like ashamed, she was thankfully not at a loss for words.

"What business have you here, Mr. Willoughby?" she addressed him with a cold formality that made him falter unbecomingly.

He was so disturbed by the lack of warm reception that instead of answering her directly, he cast his gaze here and there in distracted thought. He looked very well. That is to say, if a man ever looked well whilst suffering the deepest affliction of the soul, it was Willoughby who wore it thus. Regret had carved deeper lines in what was visible of his brow and the shadows around his mouth, marking him as one well acquainted with grief. His eyes were suited to the melancholy that had taken permanent residence within them, and he was still every fulfilment of a romantic figure that a lady might be seduced by. More so, even, as the features so full of masculine confidence had sunken to a visage that begged for comfort and consolation.

Marianne inwardly cursed him for maintaining all the outward appeal of a man who lacked every inward virtue. Elinor offered to escort Marianne inside at once and send Willoughby away with the Colonel's help if necessary, but she declined the offer, stating, "I am not afraid of him now, Elinor. I want an answer."

Still refusing her the answer she desired, in a voice hoarse and low he asked a question of his own. "Is it true?"

"Is what true?" She could not imagine he meant to question the validity of her marriage so late since its event, but a cruel foreboding chilled her heart nonetheless. "I can neither affirm nor deny your suppositions without some indication of what you desire to know; and that so desperately that you must trample upon my convenience and appear before me without warning."

"You are with child," he stated. "You cannot deny that much, for even if the rumours were to be disbelieved, the looseness of your gown betrays the truth behind your silence."

Though her cheeks turned crimson, Marianne held his gaze steadily. "What has that to do with you?"

"Is the child mine?" When she refused an answer by word of mouth, and her eyes burned fiercely in hot indignation, he accepted it as affirmation. "It is. Of course it is," he exhaled sharply. "That would explain your hasty marriage and the ridiculous duel... Why you would otherwise marry such an odious, hateful...?"

"Take care, Mr. Willoughby," Marianne rebuked, no sweetness whatever in her tone. "You are on my husband's property, slandering his good name as you address his wife."

"His good name," he jeered. "Yes, the Colonel is good, indeed, if he has not spoken of divorce and plans to raise the child here. Or does he not know? Have you tricked him into believing the child is his?"

"I do not keep secrets from my husband," she returned, then striking him a blow more crushing than any she had yet produced, "I love him too well for that."

"You cannot mean it," he said, clearly tortured by the very notion. "Marianne, you do not know what I have suffered over you. What I have suffered with a wife I do not love and could not love, for I love you alone. I love you still. Do not wound me so by making false professions, for my anguish could not be any deeper, or felt more keenly with each passing moment. My regret could not be more torturous than it is now."

"You think I pretend to love my husband in order to spite you?" Marianne realised her voice had heightened in volume, and she lowered it again to say sadly, "No, Willoughby. Your self-love must run deeper than any regret if you truly believe it possible. I love Colonel Brandon with all of my heart; the heart that you abused so thoroughly, and abandoned so quickly. We will raise the child to know *him* as its father, and you will have nothing to do with either me or the child, of that I can swear to! What was your purpose, Willoughby? Did you think to find me as miserable as you? Did you think to earn my forgiveness by speaking ill of my husband and comparing our situations? If I was inclined to forgive you, even for myself, when I consider all that the Colonel has done for me, and suffered for my sake, and continues to suffer because of my foolishness in chasing you and encouraging you, I cannot bear to even think of forgiveness."

Trembling with the onslaught of emotions, and causing Elinor to grow anxious with concern for her, Marianne decided it was time they went back to the house, and she indicated her departure by informing Willoughby he "had better go, lest she set the dogs on him."

She stood her ground with great determination until his repeated pleas were finally given up as fruitless. She continued to stand firm until he had mounted his horse and rode off with backwards glances now and then, still unwilling to fully accept that Marianne meant all that she had said to him.

When he was far beyond the grounds, and had become less than a dark smudge against the backdrop of the sky and hills, Marianne allowed Elinor to walk her home. Though she shook so violently, and stumbled so often that Elinor finally forced her to sit upon the first patch of green they came upon and ran straight to the house, calling for the Colonel all the way in a fashion most unlike her self-possessed nature.

Chapter Sixteen

Colonel Brandon had been watching at the windows for some time in anticipation of his wife's return to the house, wondering why he had not gone with her rather than allowing her only Elinor for company. The weather was fine, and gave no cause for worry, but he did not like it when the sisters slipped out of view behind the shrubbery and continued their walk beyond it so that he could not see Marianne.

Edward tried to be sympathetic, but he understood it was not the same for him. Elinor was of a much sturdier constitution than Marianne, and was also not with child. He had it from Elinor that Marianne was prone to fainting spells, and as he knew so little of them—except that his mother was forever threatening to be stricken with one as soon as things failed to align with her wishes—he could not know the fear of anticipating a genuine episode. He attempted to distract the Colonel from his incessant scowling at the empty drive and pacing to and from the view, but when all his conversations ran dry and failed to draw Colonel

Brandon's attention away from the window, he tried instead to cheer him with assurances of the sisters' safety; the agreeable weather, and Elinor's good sense and ability to care for Marianne should anything go amiss.

At such a statement, Colonel Brandon snapped his head to attention, paying heed to Edward's attempts to distract him for the first time that afternoon. "What might go amiss?" he questioned, his countenance grave and serious.

"Nothing with Elinor beside her," Edward reassured him. "I am certain they will return soon, before we set off for the chapel again."

"Marianne has little concept of time, especially when she is out walking," Colonel Brandon replied, his voice softening at the image it provided of his wife's blissful revelry in nature. "I... cannot tell you why, but I am strangely fearful for her whenever she is out of my sight. It is selfish, perhaps, to worry so relentlessly over her and place troublesome restrictions on all her favourite pursuits." He had recently begun to limit the hours she dedicated to difficult compositions, lest she weary herself with eye strain, or sit too long on the unmercifully hard piano bench. "But I have suffered great loss over the course of my life, and I am not willing to part with the most precious thing I have obtained in all my years. Not while I can do any small thing to prevent her from harm, or keep her from the slightest sorrow."

"Two precious things," Edward murmured, following his gaze out the window. "For she carries your child."

Colonel Brandon resumed his steadfast watch

and quietly echoed, "Two precious things."

A voice, unfamiliar in its pitch and urgency, carried his name to his ears, just as Elinor's form appeared below, running towards the house with no sign of Marianne in tow.

"Elinor!" Edward cried in surprise, giving no heed to where he set his half-empty glass of sherry. "That is Elinor! Elinor is... is running! Whatever can the matter be?"

Both gentlemen were upon the drive before Elinor had reached the door. Edward took her by the arms to steady her as she was quite out of breath, and Colonel Brandon waited only long enough for her to gasp out, "Marianne is quite overcome... on the lawn by the roses. She... cannot walk... Willoughby..." and he was bolting towards his wife as fast as he had ever run to escape death in battles long past.

She was cold when he reached her, and still trembling uncontrollably. He did not think it the weather that made her so, as there was more danger in browning one's complexion from lack of a proper parasol than suffering from a chill, but he removed his coat nonetheless, and wrapped her in it before lifting her into his arms and bringing her to the house.

Marianne was distraught, and her eyes wild and unseeing, but when the Colonel set her down on the chaise and made a movement that might have been interpreted as his preparing to let her go, she would not allow it, but begged hysterically that he stay with her. In her panic, she was completely unconcerned with the way she'd caused her bonnet to loosen and hang from her neck while her hair grew unruly.

"I will not leave you," he assured her, pulling her into his lap so that she might cling all the tighter to him. Despite the additional weight of the babe, he found her surprisingly light and wondered how dainty she must have been before the child had grown so. He felt a pang of envy that Willoughby had known what it was to have that delicate creature in his arms while Marianne was still untouched by his cruelty, and then a sense of triumph overruled that it was *he* who was the victor in holding both wife and child now. His "two precious things," as Edward had so innocently declared them.

Marianne was growing warmer from their closeness, but something caused her to shiver into his shirt as she said, "I lied to Elinor. I told her I was not afraid of him, but I was! I was!"

He gently tugged the length of ribbon to release her completely from the confines of her bonnet, soothing her hair as he bid her tell him what Willoughby had done. "Has he hurt you, my love? Shall I finish the job I'd begun and dispatch him to his eternal fate?"

Her head shook in the negative. "He did not hurt me, nor threaten me. Not in looks or gestures so pronounced. It is not Willoughby's way to announce his intentions to use a person ill. His manner is generally persuasive enough not to require such tactics. But still, I was so frightened."

"He is gone?" he asked gruffly, and eased somewhat to hear her whimpered assent. "I will never leave your side again," he swore.

Marianne shook her head against his chest

again. "Do not blame yourself, dear Colonel. You are not responsible for Willoughby's actions."

"I am responsible for *you*," he argued.

Knowing she would never persuade him otherwise, nor did she think it necessary to try, Marianne pushed gently against him to wrap her arms about his neck and look into his eyes for comfort. "He said that I could not love you," her voice and lip trembled in unison. "He claimed that I only pretended love in order to spite him and make him suffer. You must not believe it, Colonel!" she cried in agitation, "You must know that I am sincere when I say that I love you!"

"I know, my Marianne."

She drew some comfort from his declaring so, and her trembling became less pronounced, her voice quavered less, and her body relaxed. Still, she did not sound quite like herself as she asked, "What if he tries to take our child? What if he turns him against us?"

"Marianne, I swear to you upon my life that John Willoughby will not take our child. He relinquished any right to the child when he abandoned you both, he confirmed his unworthiness by marrying Miss Grey, and as he has no proof to make claims by, the law would also side with us. He could not be so irrational as to attempt to claim the child. It would be too much of a risk to his finally acquired assets, too damaging to his pride. He must have some sense of preservation for his own reputation."

"You are right, of course," she nodded, but still victimised her bottom lip while indulging in darker anxieties. "Willoughby loves himself too dearly to risk it all for a child—even his own flesh and blood. I was frightened for nothing."

"Anything that causes you such grief cannot be nothing," the Colonel gently reprimanded her. "And I believe Elinor would agree with me. I have never seen your sister in such evident distress before today. Shall I send for her?"

"Yes! Oh, poor Elinor to be frightened so!" Marianne in her haste removed herself from the Colonel's lap and tried to stand without assistance, promptly teetering and nearly swooning onto the floor. Colonel Brandon put a stop to her nonsense at once, telling her to stay on the couch until he brought Elinor and they would decide together how best to make Marianne at ease again.

Even in her state of dizziness, Marianne was able to tease him about tricking her into her confinement. "I will only rest until I am feeling well again. I refuse to be shut up in a room for months on end, even one as pretty and comfortable as this one."

Colonel Brandon offered her a half smile that was partially condescending, but also conveyed his willingness to forebear with his wife's insistent declarations as to how she was to spend the rest of her pregnancy—at least for the time being.

Elinor set to work seeing to Marianne's physical needs before asking any questions about the incident she had just borne witness to. Once enough pillows had been acquired—for Marianne declined the Colonel's offer to be moved to the bed—a servant was sent for tea and a few tempting sweets. Elinor settled herself in the chair Colonel Brandon had moved by the chaise so that she could sit by Marianne, and the Colonel, clearly serious about his promise not to let Marianne out of his sight, took up the remaining seat across the way. He intended on keeping himself as unobtrusive as possible, as he could sense Elinor was eager to speak with Marianne, but there was no place that would keep him far enough from hearing, yet close enough to see.

Elinor was by no means discomfited by the Colonel's presence, but took Marianne's hand in her own and asked as if they were entirely alone, "Dearest, what affected you so about Willoughby's appearance? I know you loved him once, but I had thought... you did tell me that was all past and over with. You were not moved to regret by his account, were you?"

"No, Elinor! Oh, no," she said decidedly. "Though I pity him greatly, there is no... Lingering affection—no question of anything of that nature! I was startled, though, and ill-prepared. All wretched memories of the day of his betrayal came flooding into my mind and I was unable to push them away. In my mind's eye, I could see in perfect, wretched detail the hour this child was conceived, and yet... as he stood there, brooding, and miserable, and wicked as ever he was, I still thought him handsome! I still thought him worth feelings of sincere pity! There was no temptation for me to feel anything kinder than that, but still I was overcome. I felt the pain of him anew. And I felt sick to think he might try to claim this poor child borne of violence. Our child must not know of Willoughby," she repeated. "It cannot."

Elinor paled considerably, and as she tightened

her hand to keep it from shaking, asked, "Whatever do you mean, dearest? What violence was there in your child's conception?"

Marianne studied Elinor a moment, finding it strange that she had never learned the manner of their relations in Devonshire. She supposed she had never spoken of it, and had chosen instead to bear all of Elinor's remarks against her character as testament to the irrevocable loss of her virtue as a thing deserved, but how much time had she let slip by before making it a priority to let Elinor know? After complaining to Colonel Brandon of secrets and gulfs, she felt ashamed of her hypocrisy. "I was not brought willingly to Willoughby's bed," she said at last. "I was seduced to his home, but not into his bed. Any indiscretion on my part was wrong, I know that well enough, but I did not allow him to kiss me, to touch me, to... *lie* with me as we were not yet bound by oath or covenant to each other." Elinor could not help but be aware of the way Colonel Brandon shifted in his seat, no doubt practicing the greatest self control in not rushing to Marianne's side, or verbally interjecting his loathing of the scoundrel in question.

Marianne closed her eyes and heaved a deep sigh. "I told myself afterwards that he had a right; that it was only his uncontrolled passion for me that made him unable to wait for marriage. I convinced myself that he had loved me so dearly that he could not keep himself from me, and that this act was his tragic way of bidding goodbye for the length of our separation. I truly believed we were good as engaged and he had every intention of returning to me once he'd secured his inheritance. But then his manner of departure was so swift, so... devoid of all warmth. The drive back to the party was grave and quiet. He answered only in distracted, half-smiles that worried me, but still did not warn me." Marianne stopped, frowning in silence for a moment. "Then he went to London, and though we followed soon, I dreaded the sight of him as I tried convincing myself he would come to me and makes things right. I still believed that he loved me, even then."

"Marianne..." Elinor stroked the back of her hand, hoping to show her through the action that she meant no accusation through her questioning. "You do not... think that way now, do you?"

"No. I have seen what love is through my husband," here her eyes shifted to dwell upon the quiet man across the room, and she smiled. "I have seen it in his behaviour, and in yours, Elinor. Even in Edward's, though there were moments I doubted him," she added with an attempt at levity. "I know now what Willoughby truly is, and where his heart lies, for it is not what we say or think that defines us, but what we do. Willoughby did not love me. He wanted me, perhaps, but he did not, and *does not* love me. Not in the way he should. But he has got his just desserts. You saw how miserable he is."

"I tend to think him not miserable enough."

"I tend to agree," the Colonel put darkly.

"And I do not blame either of you, but I am satisfied if he lives a long and healthy life with Mrs. Willoughby to administer the consequence of his sins all the while. I will be content, knowing the pain he will endure each time the name of our child is mentioned with the last name of Brandon as a testament to what he forsook for his current misery. Perhaps he deserves worse, but I cannot desire more than that. What I do desire is to rest, and for you both to stay near me a little while, until I am quite asleep."

This was an agreeable notion to both of Marianne's attendants, and as she slept, one watched on motionlessly from afar, and the other stayed near enough to smooth her hair and clutch her hand in intervals. Elinor had remained a quiet listener through the greater part of Marianne's recounting of her abuse, but now that there was no distraction to the murmuring of her own thoughts, she was beset by remembrances of all the harsh words she had ever judged her sister by. She could lay no blame of returning silence at Marianne's feet; she who kept so much hidden in her own heart, and spoke only of duty and principle. It was no wonder Marianne felt she could not be fully open about such an egregious attack.

It pained her to imagine all those months of suffering Marianne endured alone. Worse than alone, for Elinor had not been very kind concerning Marianne's predicament, treating it as a consequence of foolish inclinations and a weakness of character; something that required an immediate and practical solution. Now as she watched the soft rise and fall of Marianne's breaths, the pallor of her features, and considered the reaction she'd had at Willoughby's appearance only an hour past. Elinor laid her head on the edge of the chaise and wept for her poor, dear Marianne.

Much had changed since that whirlwind

courtship, both in the sisters' convictions and situations. Marianne no longer believed in saying everything on her mind at any given opportunity, and Elinor no longer was certain it was always wisest to choose prudence over passion. So long as there was a proper balance of the two, if the sisters could influence each other, they would both be the better for it.

As her tears subsided, and she was able to regain hold of her emotions once more, Elinor heard the Colonel stirring anxiously from his position across the way, and suddenly she longed for the embrace of her own husband—no doubt sequestered away in some nook downstairs, reassessing his sermon from the morning, and picking it to pieces in his solitude. Elinor dried her eyes with the handkerchief she kept always on her person, and rose to leave the Colonel to be the one Marianne awoke to.

Watching him take her previous place to tend ever so carefully to his sleeping wife, Elinor thought that it was more than the sisters who had changed for the better.

Chapter Seventeen

Colonel Brandon was growing increasingly worried regarding his wife's progressing roundness and her complete refusal to be confined. He had to admit to knowing little regarding such matters as all polite women were silent on birthing issues, and Beth had been cared for exclusively by the couple he placed her with. However, he had the word of Dr. Barnes that confinement was a necessary part of any birthing process, and it unsettled him that his wife had a blatantly opposing position than that of a long-trusted family physician.

"I can think of nothing more appalling than being shut up in a stuffy room for days on end with no sight of sunlight, nor trees, nor sky, nor anything that tempts the senses or cheers the spirit!" she declared with feeling. "How can something so dismal be a health benefit? It seems more prison than sickbed. And why should I be confined to a sickbed, even if it were so? I am not sick! I am with child! A child is not an illness to be vetted out."

"I confess, I do not understand the reason Dr. Barnes insists upon it myself, nor why it is the general procedure," Colonel Brandon admitted, "but as I am not a physician I think it best to abide by the orders of the medical professionals in such cases."

"Dr. Barnes may be a medical professional, but he is not a *Marianne* professional," she retorted. "He cannot know me better than I know myself. I informed him of how ill I became over the weeks I was shut up in my room, and he scoffed at me! He said the room must not have been dark enough, or the vapours strong enough, or the curtains thick enough. He wanted to worsen every deplorable thing about my condition! I cannot think *that* is wise." Her eyes narrowed, daring him to challenge these new offenses cast upon the doctor's character.

"Two weeks, Marianne," the Colonel sighed in surrender. "If I give you two more weeks of freedom, will you consent to your confinement?"

"I will consider it, depending on how much freedom you're offering," Marianne said with an arch of her brow. "May I play my new piece without interruption?"

His answer came somewhat delayed as he considered. "If you rest the moment you feel tired," he consented.

"May I take walks, even when it is a little chilly?" she tried.

His expression stated that he was about to refuse, but after another long pause and a deep frown at how thoroughly he was being bested at his own bargaining ploy, he said, "If you dress warmly and take an umbrella in case of rain."

"And may I entertain guests at the house?"

Such a request came as entirely unexpected to the Colonel, and his concerned tone turned to one of surprise. "What guests could you possibly desire to entertain?"

The eagerness in her voice matched that of the Colonel's surprise. "Elinor says there is a missionary from the Indies coming to see Edward. He and his friend returned to England only a fortnight ago, and they wish to stay at the parsonage." She gave him a knowing look, "You know the cottage is not very spacious for hosting additional guests, and we have rooms upon rooms to spare. It would be a great relief for Elinor if we asked them to stay here, instead."

"I have no objection to relieving your sister if it was not to shift burden onto yourself," he said cautiously. "But who is this missionary, and who is his friend that you should be so inclined to hospitality?"

"No one you would have heard of, I think," she shrugged carelessly. "Mr. Matthews is a young clergyman, and his friend is also newer to his profession. But as they come from doing a good work in the Indies, I thought that would allow you some manner of common ground. Am I not allowed to be charitable?" she asked, feigning insult. "May I not open our home to those who risk such oppressive climates and cultures to spread the Good Word to heathen nations? Colonel Brandon, you are most strange to question my motives," she teased.

"Very well," he said relenting, but jabbed a pointed finger in her direction, "Do *not* overburden yourself. Let Mrs. Pickard do the greater portion of the work. Only give minimal instructions through written menus and lists while she manages the rest."

"Even if I did over exert myself, it would be all set to rights in the end," she said blithely. "The missionary's friend is a doctor."

Colonel Brandon had no inkling of the significance of her statement until the day Mr. Matthews and his friend, Dr. McKay arrived.

Introductions were made less stilted and awkward as Edward and Elinor were there to receive their guests, though they welcomed them to Colonel Brandon's estate.

"Colonel Brandon, I believe you are familiar with Dr. McKay's charitable work among the working class mothers?" Edward said aside to him, though not so low that Marianne could not catch it.

"I confess I am not," the Colonel admitted.

"Oh. That is surprising. I would have thought Marianne eager to share with you Dr. McKay's discoveries. She and Elinor have spoken of nothing else these past weeks but his pamphlet that's been circulating around the village by the hands of Mrs. Hexom."

The Colonel furrowed his brow in contemplation. "What has Mrs. Hexom to do with Dr. McKay? I thought he was in the Indies until recently."

"Oh, he was. But Mrs. Hexom insists it was his research that decided her twins' safe delivery. It caused quite a stir among the womenfolk when she dismissed her regular physician and asked a local shepherd's wife with experience in midwifery to tend to her. Has Marianne told you none of this? I thought that the reason for their staying here instead of at the parsonage."

"My wife has told me no more than the names and occupations of the two gentlemen staying with us," he answered gruffly.

"Shall we take tea?" Marianne briskly interrupted. "We can speak of pamphlets and doctoring *after* everyone has rested and refreshed themselves."

It was not until after supper, and the gentlemen had all adjourned to the study with their drinks and conversation that the Colonel was enlightened on the matter.

Edward had asked after their work abroad, and while Mr. Matthews was encouraged by the spiritual progress, the doctor had a less optimistic view of their cultural practices. He had a great deal to say regarding the correlation between the ignorance of scriptural matters and that of health concerns, citing the ancient customs of the Israelites and their preservation from disease that plagued the nations surrounding them.

Trying to bring the conversation back to a general topic for discussion, Mr. Matthews summarised. "We've witnessed hard things, even in our short work we've begun, and it stands to reason that a lack of understanding in one aspect leads to confusion in all other areas of life."

"Precisely what I'm getting at," said Dr. McKay, not willing to let the matter drop.

"Yes, well I'm sure these gentlemen have heard enough about the appalling lack of cleanliness amongst the heathen tribes," Matthews countered.

"Not any more gruesome or heathenish than your English birthing practices," the doctor muttered, making no qualms about pronouncing the word 'English' with as much Scottish gusto as he could manage.

"McKay here has some newfangled notions about midwifery," Mr. Matthews explained to Edward and the Colonel, the latter whose interest was piqued at the doctor's sudden vehemence, feeling an unravelling of the mysteries surrounding him in his impassioned declarations.

"There is nothing natural about the way expectant mothers are confined for weeks or months on end, in stifling chambers, with no natural light or circulating air," he complained in his deep rumble. "You might as well toss them into prison and expect a happy outcome."

His words echoed Marianne's complaints in almost every particular, that it became clear from whose research she'd been influenced by.

"And this tradition of a wet nurse!" he went on, "To separate an infant from its mother in the most vulnerable stage of its growth, to be suckled by a stranger for the sake of gentility! You know what we think of the sheep who don't take their wee lambs to nurse, eh? Why do we encourage human mothers to do it?"

Mr. Matthews loudly cleared his throat. "No one can accuse you of being too genteel, John."

"You agree with me!" he cried.

"I do, for I've seen the evidence firsthand. There are certainly greater mortality rates in the babes born to wealthy mothers who are made to observe all the recommended days of lying-in. Compared to the healthier and stronger children of the working middle class who cannot afford confinement or a wet nurse, but are not so low as to be deprived of their daily bread and a clean environment. It is not only a sedentary and flagrant lifestyle that endangers the infant, nor the aloof parenting that seeks no more than the securing of an heir, but the very practices of the well-paid physicians that foolishly place the lives of their newborn patients and their mothers in great jeopardy."

"Ah," Edward murmured thoughtfully, "I had always wondered why it seemed the wealthy had fewer children. I assumed it was a strange trick of Providence, or the sheer will of the working man to have more descendants to assist in his labours."

"Or pure ignorance in how those bairns come about," Dr. McKay scoffed.

"Thoughtful in speech as always, John," chastised Mr. Matthews.

"What?" the doctor growled, crossing his arms defensively. "There are no ladies present to blush or swoon at my words. I haven't said a single vulgarity outright this whole evening!"

"No, but surely it hasn't escaped your attention that the good Colonel's wife, whose hospitality we currently impose upon is with child? Do you mean to insult him with your coarse turn of phrase?"

Whether he did or not, Dr. McKay addressed Colonel Brandon without the slightest sense of shame, "Do you intend to confine your wife? She looked rather healthy at supper. Best keep it that way if you care for her at all, and have none of this shutting-in hogwash. I've had a pamphlet printed, explaining my research and justification for my position. Maybe no one reads it now, but I'll track one down for you if you'd like."

"I care for my wife a great deal," the Colonel answered darkly, none too happy to have his affections questioned so by a young guest. "And I confess the time of her confinement has been a matter to cause some disagreement between us. But I must ask you this," he glowered seriously, "If the current procedures of our family doctors are inherently wrong, why do they persist? If—as you say—all these things are the cause of illness and death for both wife and infant, why are such practices promoted rather than altered or done away with entirely?"

Dr. McKay brightened at once, sat up straighter, and removed his boots from the settee. His eyes looked nearly wild with eagerness, almost as if waiting for this very question all the while. "Because," he pronounced, elongating the last syllable for emphasis, "the English people are too stubborn to change. They will not alter customs that have been in place for centuries, regardless of the morally abhorrent state of things, or the danger of increased mortality rates as consequence. They continue to abide by outdated and dangerous practices, because what they do is what has always been done, and no one is willing to reform."

"It is not only the British," Mr. Matthews reprimanded his heated colleague, "You forget how backwards the Indians were when we first ministered to them."

"Yes, but it was even more shocking to discover how little we've come as a civilised nation in comparison. Birthing practices here are hardly any better than there, and the heathens were willing to change the moment you showed them a better way! Is there an English man or woman in all this blessed country who would similarly react?"

Colonel Brandon did not appreciate the ironic way the doctor had pronounced the phrase, "blessed country," and he scowled menacingly at him but was deflected by a good natured grin in return.

Ever the peacemaker, Mr. Matthews stepped into the verbal fray, intent on making the unpleasant tension dissipate between his friend and his host. "Are you shocked by our modern ideas, Colonel Brandon?"

"Not at all," the Colonel replied. "It has only occurred to me why my wife was so insistent you stay here for the entirety of your visit to the Ferrars's."

"That is a welcome surprise to us," Mr. Matthews said cheerily. "Our youth and strident messages don't sit well with most elegant ladies. I am happy to know of one good lady at least, who does not scorn us without just cause. Though I daresay, it's a good thing she hadn't met my associate—and friend," he added hastily, catching the questioning expression directed at him from McKay, "before deciding to host us."

"Have you had a very bad time of it in England?" Edward questioned. "I should think you glad to be on familiar soil, amongst people who speak a language and culture you've shared since childhood."

"Not so bad as all that," he admitted. "Both countries present their own challenges and flaws.

There is a great need for ministers everywhere, and doctors, too. Not one country is perfect."

"I should think England the closest, though," Colonel Brandon said with a wry smile, and finished off his port.

Dr. McKay was good enough not to contest it, though he sorely wished to. Instead, he grumbled something about keeping still for the sake of his English mother, tipped back his own glass, and emptied its contents.

"Speaking of English mothers, we should return to the ladies," Edward uttered. "But you are welcome to my pulpit to rally support in both prayers and proselytes," he invited Mr. Matthews, who thanked him most profusely as they passed into the drawing room where the two sisters were waiting for the return of husbands and guests.

Though Colonel Brandon was prepared to be embarrassed by the subject of proper birthing measures and his apparent wrongness in trusting Dr. Barnes regarding them, such intimate discussions were not raised by Dr. McKay, who in the presence of the ladies exhibited a vast contradiction to his personality while alone with the men folk. He was all decorum and consideration, never speaking too loudly, or on any subject that might upset the more delicate sensibilities of the female persuasion. His voice was deep and robust as ever, his eyes fiery and dark as his hair and sideburns, but when coupled with the thoughtfulness he evidently was capable of when in mixed company, he proved quite a charming guest, despite the questionable accent.

If the Colonel feared Marianne's revival of the

subject, his fears went unfounded, as she allowed Elinor to feel as if the two gentlemen were hers and Edward's guests, and made no mention of advancements in medical theory, or the miserable practice of confinement.

The nearest brush he had with the topic reviving was when Marianne was asked to play, and she said it would only be a short piece as longer, more complex sonatas made her poor husband nervous for her. To which the Colonel graciously stated that he was certain Dr. McKay would have no scruples against declaring her choice of entertainment unsafe for either her or anyone else present, were it to prove so.

They spoke of it more freely in their shared chamber, when at last all guests had retired for the night, and both the Colonel and his wife were dressed in bedclothes and ready to follow suit and sleep.

"Mrs. Brandon," he began, indicating by his address that there was something intentionally playful in his speech, "You would have been most diverted to know what Dr. McKay has to say on the subject of confinement."

"Oh?" she smiled prettily, barely looking up from her book of sonnets she kept at the bedside table, and the Colonel found it a great struggle to continue with as much levity as he'd begun.

Rather than spare himself the temptation, Colonel Brandon climbed into bed beside his wife and loomed rather impressively over her, close enough to catch the scent of her fragrance as he said, "There's no need to feign surprise. I'm well aware of how you and Elinor conjured up this visit on the premise of Edward and Mr. Matthews to share fellowship and flock. It seems you are to have an extension on your two weeks of freedom, my dear."

"Am I?" she asked, surprised by how weakly pronounced it was as she considered this her triumph. The sudden lack of space between them overwhelmed her and she attempted to set the book aside without appearing too eager to have the remaining space filled.

"Yes," he whispered, and the port wine he enjoyed before bed carried over on his breath, making her thrill strangely. Or perhaps it was the meaningful gleam in his eyes that affected her so.

It was a rare moment when Marianne experienced such feelings that she could find no words to properly express them, but now was such a time, and she could offer no better sign of her gratitude than to lean forward and close the gap between them in order to kiss her husband properly.

Chapter Eighteen

Colonel Brandon answered her kiss with a gruff response that took Marianne by surprise. Although he was visibly and certainly affected by her voluntary show of affection, he broke it off in order to assess her full intentions. Her expression was eager; her cheeks flushed a rosy hue, her eyes lively, and perhaps, if he was not misjudging her, there was even a sign of lust in their warm depths.

"Do you mean to soothe my losses in the breaking of our agreement?" His eyes narrowed hungrily, "I feel some compensation is certainly due since I am forced to yield."

A strange and wonderful thrill coursed through Marianne as her husband's breath lingered on her lips. He may have broken their kiss, but he seemed perfectly able to converse in such close proximity that it drove her to frustration not to continue. "Do you mean..." she swallowed slightly, "Shall we... that is to say," she stumbled over her words, not at all assured of how she might go about clarifying the act she wished to experience with her husband without sounding crass. "The woman *did* say it was safe."

"I only meant that instead of confinement, you should spend your evenings with me, rather than with Elinor in the drawing room, guests or no guests. If we are to break tradition, we should be quite thorough with it, do you not agree?"

"I do," she murmured, "And I believe I can think of something even more scandalous to spend our evenings doing, rather than carrying on polite conversation and then slipping into separate beds." Her hand slipped down to the gap in his nightshirt and her eyes trailed down the same path.

"Marianne," he shuddered as a new sensation coursed over him through her touch, "that is not what I meant. We cannot..."

"On whose authority do you claim that we cannot join properly as man and wife?" she complained. "Is it not only desirable but scriptural? Do not make me call on Edward for his pastoral sanction." Marianne raised an eyebrow in challenge. "Or am I wrong to suggest consummation is mutually desirable in this case? Am I much too plump now to be pleasing to you?"

Colonel Brandon's scoff which came from deep in his chest sounded almost like a growl. "You know nothing could be further from the truth."

"How could I know that when my husband refuses to lie with me?"

The Colonel carefully took stock of his wife's playful pout, the fingers that still toyed with the opening at his shirt, and found it very difficult to still ask, "Will you not be frightened? Or uncomfortable?" He lowered his eyes to the slight but still visible lump beneath her shift. "I cannot...

lie with you as is customary because of your condition. What if I harm the babe?"

Marianne toyed with the bottom of her lip, catching it between her teeth as she thought how to form her suggestion. "If it is not entirely reprehensible to you, I had thought to join with you in a way that would be more comfortable for me, though far less customary as I understand."

"I am almost afraid to ask," he said playfully, eyes narrowed in suspicion.

Marianne gave a short, impatient laugh. "It merely requires a reversal of positioning. If you promise not to be *very* scandalised that I know such a practice exists, and do not ask me from whom I learned such a thing, I will be very glad to show you."

Not allowing him the time to object any further, Marianne pushed against her husband's chest to indicate she wished for him to give her the space to sit up. As he sat further back, and she moved forward, she began to kiss him quite liberally, and without any pretence of restraint. Her hands were not idle, either, as they smoothed over his temple and found purchase in his hair. She smiled to herself in thinking of how very foolish she had been to ever consider him aged. Though the lines of care and loss were etched firmly in his face, the arms that caught hold of her were strong and muscular; his hair full and tawny, not yet brushed by the silver of those who might truly claim old age.

The Colonel himself was so caught up by her continuous ministrations that he hardly noticed when she pushed him to a reclining position against the pillows and situated herself comfortably on top of him.

Rather than be bothered by such a forward gesture, he found the weight of her quite pleasing, especially as she ever so slowly and torturously slid her hips further down his torso, continuing her trail of kisses on his face and neck all the while.

Colonel Brandon suffered a fleeting lapse of worry that there might be something strange or unholy in their current situation, but being that his lovely wife was not only claiming to be comfortable this way, but also by the telling sighs and flushed cheeks between her proffered kisses, *enjoying* the interlude as deeply he was, the worry was quick in passing. He gave up the fight altogether when she took his hands to guide them under the folds of her shift and over the gooseflesh of her thighs which were more and more exposed as the garment insisted on hiking further up her legs with every downward motion. He would certainly not complain. She was as soft and warm as he had imagined, striving not to think of what it must be like to run his hands upon such intimate places whenever she slept beside him and the covers were thrown off during the course of a warmer evening. Now she was quite awake with no covers whatever to impede his explorations while she offered her body for him to touch as he pleased and all temptation could be readily acted upon.

It seemed impossible, but Marianne gave him even greater agony as she slid yet further down, leaving only the length of his nightshirt and a few more inches for them to truly join.

It was not instantaneous; not hurried, nor

frenzied, but after some moments of her repeated explorations, when she had discovered the delightful reaction she produced by skimming her hands over his chest beneath the folds of his nightshirt, and found her own pleasure to increase by the evidences of his, the urge for them to join grew more dire, and he pressed her firmly, one hand on either side of her hips to indicate he wished for her to complete the downward path she had begun.

When at last she did, when she enveloped him and welcomed him fully, he could not restrain himself from keeping a watchful eye on how she moved over his body. At first, he watched from the lingering fear that some foul memory would suddenly take hold of her and ruin their intimacy. However, as the moments passed and it was clear Marianne had banished all coherent thought in favour of enhancing the pleasure she derived from her increasingly forceful motions, he too put aside needless worry and watched her solely for his own pleasure. For he did consider it wonderful to be taken by such a woman, and in such a way; never would he have imagined so willing a wife in marital congress, and certainly not the object of his long-held affections not only accepting, but *insisting* upon their union.

She was loveliness itself; curls so like his in colour rapidly loosening from their braided confinement to fall unheeded over her forehead and brushing against her cheek, beaded with the perspiration of her exertions. Though her shift had slipped off to one side so that much of her shoulder and part of her breast was tantalisingly revealed,

Colonel Brandon was of the opinion that it was not revealing enough, and acting upon pure desire, he loosened the laces as hastily as he could and pulled the shift down so that both her breasts were exposed in the faint light provided by the bedside candle.

Marianne shivered, and he immediately felt sorry, imagining her to be shivering from the cold air she was forcibly exposed to. However, she smiled down at him and cheekily suggested he might try his hand at warming them.

"Ah!" she cautioned, as he hastened to do so, "but gently, my love, as they have been somewhat sensitive of late."

Taking his commission most seriously, he did his utmost to both provide warmth, and yet not pain his wife in the meantime. Soon, he had struck up a most pleasant approach that satisfied both desires, and he forewent any further thought of repentance as both he and his wife revelled in the contact.

The knowledge—nay, the proof that she desired this, desired *him*, was more than he could bear, and as his own desire overcame him, he adjusted his hold on her, afraid to cling too tightly to part of Marianne for fear he might hurt her in the expenditure of his passion.

When he was sated, he determined that she should experience the same, but Marianne withdrew from him with a merry laugh. "You needn't worry on my account. I have had my share of pleasure tonight."

"Are you certain?" he frowned, disappointed by the return of her shift to its usual place over her shoulders and other, more appealing parts of her anatomy.

"You were not exactly attentive at the time I had..." even now she blushed, and Colonel Brandon did not think she could be any more beautiful than she was in her currently dishevelled and self-conscious state, the wildness of her hair and rumpled nature of her shift lingering evidences of what they had just shared.

Colonel Brandon rose to bring them towels from the basin so that they might wash themselves into a more respectable state before settling back into bed. Out of habit, they both assumed their usual stations, he on one side, she on the other. The Colonel lay there in the silence for a time, blissfully tired and ready to welcome sleep, except for the disappointment he felt over their current arrangement. He wanted to draw her close and hold her to him as he slept, but worried that she might find such a sleeping position distasteful. Perhaps she would rather sleep with the space between them. He doubted that the woman who had just shown such boldness in their relations could possibly be too embarrassed to voluntarily push herself into his embrace, but it was folly to assume anything when it came to the inclinations of his wife.

He lay there in the black silence for a time, the candlelight having been extinguished already and leaving him in darkness to wonder blindly. Several times he nearly turned on his side to prod her and ask if she slept, but could not muster up the courage to do so.

The strange and discontented silence was

broken by the faintest of sniffles, and when he
stayed very still, he could discern movement from
his wife's side as she shook from trying to suppress
her crying.

"Marianne?" he spoke softly into the dark and
the word seemed only to worsen her distress, for it
brought forth the hitherto stifled sobs. She could no
longer muffle the cries, or force herself to still the
shaking at the sound of his voice. "My dear love,"
he said, distraught, placing what he hoped was felt
as a comforting hand on her shoulder, purposing to
touch the part covered by her shift in case direct
contact with his flesh was unwanted.

She turned in the bed, but it was not to shake off
his hand, or create more distance between them as
he feared. Instead, she moved through the
blackness to sidle into his embrace, and in such a
way that the babe's dwelling space was not
impeded.

"I thought you had gone to sleep, just as you
were, as we always do," she explained, voice
wavering with the effects of her crying. "It was so
quiet, and I... I was lonely. I did not want to sleep
so very far away from you, after what just passed
between us. It seems as though things should be
different, now we are truly married, but then it was
not, and I..." He had not the time to call her foolish
and assure her he felt the same bereavement
without her presence in his arms, for she kept on,
"And, also... I feel so much in this moment that I do
not know if I *can* sleep tonight. My mind is very
cruel to me."

"Then you must tell me how it is so and I will
rebuke it," Colonel Brandon promised, gently

running his hand over her head as if to show how he meant it.

She shrank into the covers, as if ashamed of what thoughts came to her unbidden. "I cannot help but feel pain in the knowledge that I am... that this was not..." Her voice grew even softer, and the Colonel would have strained to hear her, had he not been perfectly still and silent while she spoke. "It is that I am with child, and the child is not yours, and you did not take for yourself a pure and honest girl to bed properly for the first time."

He let out a long breath, meant to give him time to form the proper response. "Marianne," he said at last, "I chose to take you as my wife, knowing full well the measure of your history. In living with you and knowing you better through these past months, I have only been granted more affirmation of my choice being the greatest furtherance of my happiness. I would rather you and your child than the most spotless innocent. You must know this. You cannot have continued ignorant for so long. If I hesitate to embrace you it is for fear that I care more deeply—that I will always love you more than you could love me, and I do not wish to force myself upon you, no matter how severely I pine for you. I tell myself I must wait. Wait for you to show one more sign, to speak and tell me I may kiss you, may hold you, and then wait for yet another sign that you will not detest me for it after."

"How tragic!" she murmured against him and her trembling voice was tragic, indeed. "How we both have only caused ourselves and each other more suffering by our forced temperance. I have given you every reason to doubt my affections from the beginning of our acquaintance, I know. But they are real, now, dear husband. Do you not believe me?"

"I... perhaps in time will learn to put my doubts aside, but you must be patient with me as I have tried to be with you."

"I shall," she agreed, now sighing more comfortably. "And I shall remember to tell you often that you may kiss me, and hold me, and stroke my hair as you are now, and speak softly very close to my ear, and tell you when you have that I am quite happy for you to have done so."

He hummed contentedly into her hair, sleep threatening to steal over him again, but one niggling question still refusing to let him succumb.

"Are you quite settled, wife?"

Marianne yawned in a way that forced her whole frame to stretch, and by the strength of it, it seemed the night had thoroughly exhausted her.

"Then you should sleep," he insisted, planting yet another kiss on her forehead.

She made no verbal reply, but took his arm to wrap it more securely around her in a position that kept her both close and comforted, and that way, she slept.

Chapter Nineteen

Spring drifted by in a succession of happy nothings. Marianne felt that though she and her Colonel experienced their honeymoon weeks much later in their marriage than most couples, there was nothing wanting in the ways they sought to make up for the past. There had never been a time that Colonel Brandon might have been accused of being inattentive to his wife, but he pursued her with a renewed joy that could only come of receiving and returning love free of doubts and distraction. Everyone remarked on his youthful expression, the lightness in his step, and how well marriage suited him in every way. There was a tendency towards mirth that had been previously unseen in the Colonel, and those that knew him well were gratified to notice it. That Marianne found her happiness in forming his, was equally the persuasion and delight of each observing member of their familial acquaintance. She would never be as prudent or settled in disposition as Elinor, but it was her open affability and eagerness in her husband's company that gave him such joy, and his seriousness and stability anchored her otherwise unbounded nature.

The business of her care during the last four months of her condition were carefully attended to by a midwife who came recommended by Mrs. Pickard, and whose knowledge and capabilities were well investigated by Dr. MacKay before he followed his friend back to the Indies for their charitable work for the impoverished there. Though the Colonel's original prerogative was to begrudge any and all orders of Dr. MacKay, the proof of his wisdom found in Marianne's good health, and his subsequent departure from that country made it far easier for the Colonel to accept his newfangled notions and allow Marianne the freedom she craved.

Summer came upon the little cottage of Elinor and Edward just as it did for those at the Great House, though the manner of its approach differed for the two households. Along with a good crop of strawberries and a most surprising excess of dairy products from the Ferarrs's cows came the news that Elinor was in the family way. She had none of the inducements to lie-in from her husband as Marianne had at first, for even if the inclination to have her do so had come upon him in some inexplicable brain fever, it was impossible for their livestock and crops to be properly tended to without her constant labour. When economies allowed, they did hire a village boy to help with the more strenuous tasks, but the majority of the work must be done by Elinor, and she would have it no other way. Besides, she did not trust the village boy, and though she could not say precisely what caused her mistrust, she was certain there was something sly in the nature of his doings. He did not cheat them, kept strictly to his hours, and worked well and hard, but he seemed more interested in the happenings at Delaford than one would consider entirely natural from a field hand's son. Elinor asked him once if he knew the Colonel, or her sister, Marianne at all, or if he had any dealings with them that would cause such a curiosity, but he turned such a violent shade of red and denied the charge so emphatically that she ceased to pester him about it, afraid she had embarrassed him dreadfully, and decided that foolish paranoia might be a symptom from her maternal condition.

Mrs. Dashwood, who never lost her favouritism for Marianne, found a new purpose in fussing over Elinor and her situation, and she would stay at the Great House as much to find ways for her and Margaret to alleviate some of Elinor's burdens as to be near Marianne through her last months of expecting.

It was mid-morning on one fine summer day when Marianne felt the distinct pains and rush of expelling fluid to announce that the time drew near for her child to be born. It was near the hour when Mrs. Dashwood was wont to set off for the parson's cottage, but Marianne's predicament kept her from donning hat and shawl, and she hastened instead to be by her side and fulfil any requests of her daughter that the attending maid was unqualified to take care of, or the midwife unable.

Margaret stayed sulking in her room, for she was not needed to tend to Marianne, nor was she able to walk to Elinor's without someone to escort her. Her mother tried in vain to tempt her out of doors if only to play with the dogs, but Margaret had been looking forward to learning Elinor's recipe for Shepherd's Pie and was stubbornly inconsolable. Mrs. Dashwood soon gave up on her and left her to her own devices while she saw to Marianne. Elinor was sent for with the understanding that she was to come only if she could possibly be spared from home. She arrived within the hour.

Colonel Brandon took up a post outside the door, pacing to and fro like a madman, until Marianne asked after him enough times for the midwife to permit his presence. Marianne sat very near the edge of the bed; eyes shut, hands on her belly, and grimacing against what appeared to be a severely unpleasant sensation. She was in one of the spare rooms; close as any chamber was to the linen closet and kitchen. The posts of the bed had strong tassels tied to it, presumably for Marianne to grasp hold of, should the pain be more than simply grimacing could endure. Elinor sat behind her as a support, speaking to her quiet encouragements now and then when she thought it fitting.

The midwife gave the Colonel a sharp look as he entered, placing a sheet over Marianne's previously exposed thighs. Colonel Brandon graciously withheld his scoffing. There was nothing of Marianne he had not seen before in their intimacy, and it was absurd to assume modesty at such a time as this. When Marianne's pains had dissipated for the time being, she greeted her husband with far more welcome than the midwife.

"They tell me you are not to be here," she said wearily, though seemingly more at peace to see him near, "but I am stubborn and insisted. Though Mrs. Clintock says she may throw you out at any moment."

This produced a snort from the midwife. "So long as he stays well out of my way, I'll try to tolerate him. A husband in the birthing room," she shook her head. "Never heard of such a thing."

Colonel Brandon attempted to show his goodwill by not answering her in like manner. He wished to be of some *use* to his travailing wife, but could find no employ that was not already taken up by Mrs. Dashwood, Elinor, or Mrs. Clintock for obvious reasons. He did not see that he did any more good standing stoically by while Marianne suffered so terribly than he had done by pacing outside the chamber, but after each of her bouts with the intensifying labour pains, she would search for a glimpse of him and seem to draw some kind of solace merely by seeing that he still stood by. By and by, he did draw up a chair, and felt a little less foolish sitting out of the way of the bustling women while remaining close enough for Marianne's comfort.

When the time for delivery drew nigh, and Marianne was instructed to shift to the edge of the bed so that she might begin the most exhausting process of delivering the child, Colonel Brandon spent the majority of those hours wringing his hands and offering silent prayers to the heavens. If *he* felt as if this day would never end, he could hardly imagine what poor Marianne suffered.

She had been pushing for some time, and was

very close to delivery when the midwife demanded to know why the maid was taking so long with the fresh supplies she'd asked for nearly a quarter of an hour ago. Mrs. Dashwood hurried to find the maid and urge her on, but rather than find the girl she sought, another maid was almost collided with, begging to know where the Colonel might be.

The commotion could be heard outside the chamber as the door was left ajar, and Mrs. Dashwood's shrill exclamation was loud enough to be carried to Marianne's ears.

"Whatever the matter is, it can wait. See to it that the linens are brought up at once! The Colonel cannot speak to you now, as he attends his wife who is ready to have his child at any moment!"

There was an intelligible answer from the maid — her voice not being nearly as insistent or her tone as authoritative as Mrs. Dashwood's, but the returning queries made it clear what had harried the maid so.

"Why should Willoughby be here?! He has no business with my daughter any longer! And certainly not at such a time as this! Tell him to be off! And for heaven's sake, *bring me those linens!*"

The nature of this revelation sent Marianne into a near fit of hysterics, and the rosy hue in her cheeks caused from her exertions was turned a sickly white. "He is come for the child!" she said wildly, already panting heavily with labour. "He will take our little one!" Thus saying, she clutched at the tassels and groaned as another pain came upon her and the midwife encouraged her to push again. When she had done, the frightful exclamations began anew that Willoughby intended on snatching their child away, and the Colonel feared she would work herself into such a state that might cause danger to either herself or the infant she currently struggled to bring into the world.

Elinor also tried to soothe her sister, and redirect all her effort into the birth of her child, but she would not be persuaded to any semblance of calm until Colonel Brandon swore to take care of the matter and left her with Elinor for support, and Mrs. Dashwood who had finally discovered the missing maid and extra linens.

The Colonel made his way out to the foyer, where Willoughby had forced his way in, causing the maid who had been pushed aside the greatest distress. She knew it was not her station to open the door, but Mr. Meren was helping Sophie and the others access all the locked cupboards to collect supplies for the midwife, and he could not be spared in that moment, so she had gone to see who was there, but the gentleman had pushed his way right through, and she was terribly ashamed, but "please don't sack me, sir."

Colonel Brandon assured the maid she was in no danger of losing her place, and sent her to help the others in any capacity she was able. Though his words were gentle, there was a hardness in his tone that was easily explained by the venomous look he was bestowing upon the unwanted guest in his home.

Willoughby's nervous demeanour and dishevelled appearance bespoke of his harried journey there, and the knowledge he had of some emergency, though how he might possibly come to know the time that Marianne was about to give birth, Colonel Brandon could hardly imagine.

Willoughby opened his mouth to speak the first word, but the Colonel stopped him short by striking a heavy blow to his mouth. He raised him from the ground with a strong grip on his poorly kempt shirt, and dragged him towards the door from where he meant to throw him out onto the gravel.

"M... Marianne..." Willoughby sputtered, his words thick from his newly swollen cheek and mouth filling with blood. "Is she well?"

"My *wife* is none of your business," the Colonel growled, "and if you do not leave this property and swear never to return, I will finish the job I began when I challenged you for her honour."

"I must know," he begged desperately, not bothering to rise from the prostration Colonel Brandon's evicting him from the house had reduced him to. "I must know she is well and... and the child is safe. Please, I beg of you. I am but dust and ashes before you," he grovelled pitifully. "I have tried every tactic imaginable just to hear word of her. I even hired a village boy to keep me informed, should anything befall her! Only tell me she is well, Brandon! I beg of you!"

Hateful as the man before him was, ruinous as he'd been to the women Colonel Brandon cared for, he was not entirely impervious to Willoughby's wretched pleadings, and told him, "She is overtaken by fits whenever she knows you are near. That is all I will tell you of the matter. That is all the answer I will grant you. Prolonging your stay is a danger to both her and the child she struggles to bring into this world. You know I am not a jesting man, and I intend to make good on my threat if you do not leave our home at once."

"Will you not send me word when the worst of it is over? Can you not pity me at all? Enough for the smallest of notes! I must know she lives."

"The time has long passed since you had any right to know what befalls her. You shall know of her fate no sooner than the rest of those too far outside our acquaintance to warrant direct contact."

"And the child?"

"Belongs to me."

Willoughby's expression was one of such confusion, that the Colonel almost thought he'd been struck mute. He regained his faculties enough to sputter, "You... you cannot mean to... You really mean to raise...?"

"Willoughby," the Colonel uttered through partially clenched teeth, "though you may find it beyond your capacity to care for other men's offspring, including the fatherless daughters you so readily abuse and abandon for your own pleasure, I am not so basely inclined and will gladly raise the child as my own son or daughter, despite the unfortunate truth of their begetting. The world will know the child as mine, sparing Marianne any blight on her reputation, and you will have no part in its life, or ours for as long as you remain living."

He did not wait for an answer. Having made it abundantly clear that he had every advantage over Willoughby in situation, legal prowess, and even personal happiness, the Colonel strode back into his grand home, and shut the door on the rouge outside.

Returning to the spare chamber, nursing only a moderate pain in his knuckles, he was struck with a great and sudden foreboding as he approached the shadow of the threshold. The heavy door had been left open, and an unnatural silence had befallen the room. For a bleak moment, the breath left his lungs, the ability to move forsook his limbs, and he knew true terror at the pounding of his heart that throbbed in his chest. What the silence meant, he dared not imagine. He could not even pace, could not even open his mouth to request some sign of life from within. Something like a cat's mewl reached his ears, and it was followed by the gentle noise of feminine laughter.

"Colonel!" Elinor exclaimed as she hurried out the door with an armful of soiled linens, "You mustn't be afraid of her! Go in and meet your daughter!"

He passed the watchful midwife and the gore of afterbirth without hesitation. He had eyes only for Marianne and her wellbeing, although his attention was distracted by the tiny, wrapped bundle she held in her arms. Marianne's brow was furrowed, though in deep fascination rather than fear or consternation; she was pale, but not fearfully so. Her eyes were bright and merry, no longer wild, her mouth slightly ajar as she stared at what she held. "Where is the Colonel?" she murmured, almost as if to the bundle itself, "Where is my husband?"

"I am here, my love," he intended to announce, but the words came forth in a reverent whisper.

She looked up at him, eyes filling with tears, though she was no longer in distress. Willoughby was entirely forgotten in the joy she derived from that small, wrapped thing in her arms. "I wished to be certain of you," she said. "Come and take my hand. It is easier when you hold me like this. Tell me all will be well, dearest. Tell me we will love her, and not ever let on that hers was a painful beginning."

He stared into the round, pink face of Marianne's daughter — *their* daughter — and wondered at the softness of her cheeks, the daintiness of her features, and the serenity of her expression under such conditions as being newly born. He felt his heart twist with a new dread as he gazed at the tiny girl. How could he call himself a man worthy of this child and her mother's love if he ever let anything befall her? The thought of it made him reel, and he was forced to tighten his squeeze on his wife's hand to chase away the prospect of such a thing.

"Never," he declared. "She shall know no hurt if I can do anything in my power to prevent it. I swear to you, I will always take care of you both. Our Mary will never want for anything."

"Mary," she breathed, and rubbed her nose against the babe's own, being that her hand was still securely clutched in the Colonel's and not free for petting her little one. Mary's nose crinkled at the contact, and she mewed again, this time a little louder; perhaps even angrily at the disturbance. "It is not so different from 'Marianne,' is it?" she teased. Then speaking to her daughter directly, she said, "Did you hear your Papa, Miss Minney Brandon? You shall be cared for always. For you are ours to love, and we shall love you well."

Epilogue

No one but the Colonel, and perhaps in some ways, Marianne, was prepared for the succession of children to follow Mary's birth. It was not that the general populace had trouble understanding why Colonel Brandon and his young wife might wish to fill their many grand and spacious rooms with smaller people of their own — less civil tongues may have wagged at a desire to continue populating until an heir to the estate was acquired — and certainly no one was in a better position to provide for so many dowries; but four girls in a row, all surviving infancy and beyond was something of a welcome miracle to the gentry.

The dear people were more than happily resigned to the fate of raising four daughters, and with the trials of the Dashwood family's past still impressed upon Marianne, and through her history, the Colonel, the latter knew and understood the significance of laying up for each of his girls to be well looked after in the event of his death, regardless of how well off their prospective husbands might turn out to be.

The Colonel was most verbally adamant, despite his generosity to his daughters, that he would find suitable husbands for them all when the time came.

"I should be on the lookout for young men of good character and morals," he remarked from his chair, quite unprompted as he and Marianne watched their young daughters at play, the newest of them all sleeping easily in her mother's arms, undisturbed by the low conversation and familial noises.

His wife observed his dark expression, thinking it wholly disconnected from the gentle scene before them. Just as all lively children, the girls had their disagreements and unpleasant rows from time to time, but this evening all seemed content to play amiably together, or at least break away without complaint if the activities of another sibling didn't quite suit their interests.

Ellen had created a village by arranging wooden blocks into towers and rows, while baby Sarah sat up against Duke's warm belly, fascinated by the sound made by repeatedly knocking two of the blocks together. Mary observed Ellen's workmanship with a judging eye for a while, offering better ideas for proper stacking in a tone that suggested superior wisdom, but she soon gave up on her younger siblings entirely to build more impressive towers a few yards away, unrestrained by faulty architecture.

Marianne bestowed a feather-light kiss on their youngest daughter's downy head before answering her husband. She never tired of watching Nan as she slept. She thought all of her daughters had been pretty infants, but Nancy seemed the first to take after her father in looks, possessing more aquiline features than the others as infants, and she was more thrilled than she could say to think the delicate face would form into a distinguished, noble one like Colonel Brandon's. Her eyes, too, already held a seriousness and depth about them that she hoped persisted until adulthood.

She could not think of a more worthy way to spend an evening than here with her Colonel and their daughters. She could not even recall the last time she demanded poetry or a romantic novel to while away the time. It was felicity enough to hear the Colonel read a pretty faerie story to the girls, or explain in small words how this or that creature they were curious about liked to live and eat. She felt as if she was happiness itself as she surveyed the occupants of that cosy room.

Her husband, however, was still scowling.

"You look quite serious, my dear," she remarked, somewhat amused by his pensive mood.

"I am," he stated, never taking his eyes away from the children. "I will not have their affections toyed with, or their hearts broken by ill-intentioned scoundrels."

Her teasing tone faltered, and she tried to answer him in similar brevity. "Minney is only six years old, and Nanny is not even a month born, but you are already anxious over their husbands?"

"I have no wish to delay preparations until we are caught off guard."

Marianne rose with some difficulty to lay the sleeping babe into the Colonel's arms, confident that contact with his daughter would ease some of the lines forming in his brow. And though it did, he did not venture a smile until she also knelt by the chair to kiss his cheek. Only then was he stirred from his anxious reverie to attend her fully, and let the smile return to his face once more.

"You are still comparing their situation to what mine was," she warned him, "and though you are good to be wary, you forget one very important detail. Our girls have something to their advantage which I was deprived of."

"Sufficient dowries?"

Marianne tried to contain the volume of her laughter so as not to wake her smallest one. "No, my love! I mean a present father who will temper any romantic sensibilities with good sense and proper discipline."

"You make me sound quite the taskmaster," he grumbled, but without any real petulance. It was near impossible to be gruff with his hand occupied in stroking the softest cheek that ever was. He thought Nan looked like she might take after him in looks, and he was struck with a strange combination of pride and pity.

"Far from it," she murmured, smoothing away the remaining creases of worry in his expression with a gentle hand, "You are the kindest and best of fathers."

"I have no wish to spoil them," he said in an unnecessary defence, sighing slightly from the concerns he bore.

"No, we have all seen the effects of a spoiled child." She meant it in reference to their wretched cousin, Harry Dashwood, spawned from the loins of John and Fanny, though the Colonel was dwelling more despondently on a ruined girl of long ago who saw the ill effects of his own overindulgence.

"We have not had any sons, though," she sighed. "We might not know how to raise a son properly if we had one."

The Colonel turned his head upwards to smile fondly at her. "I do not mind having all daughters. Especially if they all grow to be as fine and beautiful as their mother."

"You had better hope they learn to be better and wiser than their mother, or it will be the young men you'll be warning away from *them*."

He opened his mouth to protest, to tell her it was so unlikely a man would exist to be worthy of any of his daughters that the very thought was preposterous, but just at that moment, Sarah let out a bone-rattling sneeze, frightening Ellen into knocking over her city of blocks, and Mary to squeal in laughter. Faithful Duke, though momentarily startled, barely flinched at the babe's unexpected outburst, and promptly went back to dozing on his paws the moment it was certain there was no real threat to his ladies.

Sometime after they had discussed and decided on how they might make provision for each of their girls—as if it was expected that they would likely produce *only* daughters—another addition to the family was born. This time, a son. Nancy was all of five years and eight months when her brother was born, and was old enough to claim upon his arrival that the small, round-headed creature was hers by right, no matter how Mama or Nurse might protest.

His name thereafter was Boy. That is to say, his parents who were generally reasonable people christened him Peter, but friends and acquaintances took to calling him "the Brandon boy," as if to distinguish him further from the flock of sisters preceding him. Nanny found this quite an acceptable title, and easy for her young lips to pronounce, and her elder sisters were so enchanted with her adoption of his nickname that they adopted it as well. "Boy" hardly knew his proper name for the remainder of his life.

In contrast to the succession of offspring from the Great House, Edward and Elinor, through no fault of their own, had a more sensible amount of children. Having first produced a male child and thereby securing their own claims to the Ferrars lineage, they had a girl three years after, and God, it seemed, was pleased to let that be the completion of their family.

This was, admittedly, something of a relief to Elinor, who although never minding the necessity of economising was not ignorant of the fact that their little cottage would not comfortably support very many occupants. She had more sleepless nights than she liked to admit over the impossibility of affording an addition to the house in the foreseeable future. It was with mixed feelings, then, that she took the news that she was not likely to have any more children after the birth of their daughter. Edward was, as always, most content with his family's situation, no matter the case.

In general, it could be said that all was as it should have been, though Marianne was periodically nettled by fears relating to her eldest daughter's begetting. For a time, she worried that

Mary's pale beauty and dark eyes were so like John Willoughby's that it would alert the entire village of their relation, or worse, that Minney would discover some inexcusable difference between herself and her sisters, and be ruined forever in the discovery. Colonel Brandon had nothing to say that would dissolve her fears until Ellen was a little grown with the same dark eyes and fair complexion as her sister, and if that were not enough, Sarah also bore characteristics that were clearly not passed down from her father.

Though the danger of being singled out as having a questionable place in the Brandon line was never truly pressing, Mary did come to be known as a remarkable beauty, even more so than any of her sisters, and there were, at times, something in her look, and especially her profile, marks of expression that were neither Marianne's nor Colonel Brandon's, but belonging to the man they hoped she would never know as her progenitor.

Willoughby never came to them again. At least, they were not accosted by him at any time that the Colonel or Marianne was aware of. This could have been a testimony to the Colonel's overprotective ways, or perhaps it was merely the wisdom of Willoughby biding his time that saw so many years without his intrusion. The fact that they could never be entirely certain that he would let them alone for good did continue to plague Marianne, though as the years wore on, she grew less and less fearful.

Aunt Margaret was a favourite among the children, being grown enough to mind them in place of Marianne or the governess, but not so grown that she'd forgotten the best games and amusements for spirited young people.

Mary Brandon outgrew such frivolities almost before her aunt, preferring conversation on tangible matters to anything make-believe could inspire. She was as interested in her father's books and business as she was in her mother's running of the household, and considered it her God-given duty to uphold the honour and respectability of their family unit. It was Minney with her calculating judgements who harboured the most misgivings against Mr. Richard Abbott throughout his courtship of her Aunt Margaret, and it was Minney who was the most enthused about their marriage once he had proven himself a worthy officer and gentleman. Though she was but six years of age during her aunt's courtship, her opinions on such matters were clearly stated and unfaltering in duration.

As she grew, the Colonel gradually amended his standards of a match for her, convinced by the time she was eleven that the man she would marry must not only be upright, kindly, and well-mannered, but also possessing of an impressive title.

"Our Miss Brandon must have a lord," he decided, and Mary never said anything to the contrary. In fact, if her father had not required such virtues to be present in her pursuers, she would have insisted upon them herself.

Before Miss Brandon had come of age, or a lord could be found for her to care whether or not she ever came out, the Brandon Boy had made his appearance, and Mary took it upon herself to instruct him in all matters pertaining to the responsibilities of the estate as well as the particulars of proper gentlemanly behaviour. She and Nan were often rivals for Boy's attention, as the one was relentless in what she deemed necessary character growth, and the other would not participate in anything at all unless her Boy could be spared to join in.

Their brother was a good-natured lad who was as fond of his doting sisters as they were of him, though perhaps a little less aggressive in demeanour than Mary might have hoped for the Brandon heir. Still, he was by no means a disappointment, and once they'd all grown used to having a brother, all the Miss Brandons—and their parents as well—settled into their lives with as much joy and purpose as one ought to expect of a thriving family of seven.

There was an occasion or two past her coming out in which Mary was approached by a tall and handsome gentleman of about her mother's years, who attempted to make an introduction of himself. Being wary of strangers in general, and insulted by his lack of decorum in not waiting for a proper introduction by way of a mutual friend or acquaintance, Mary had none of it, refusing to even acknowledge his existence except to ask her Aunt Margaret what sort of ill-mannered rogue might behave so presumptuously. Upon receiving a full description of the gentleman in question, Aunt Margaret grew uncharacteristically serious.

"That sounds like Mr. Willoughby," she said, "He was very fond of your mother once."

"Why should he take an interest in me?" Mary

questioned. "It must have been very long ago that he was fond of Mama."

"Perhaps he has not got over her, still. I was younger than you when it all came about, but there was a time when it seemed... well," she faltered, not wanting to give her niece the wrong impression if her memory was faulty, "What I do know of the matter is that he broke your mother's heart, and your father married her to mend it."

Mary raised an eyebrow disbelievingly, "That sounds like one of your contrived romances. How could Mama have her heart broken by a man she did not marry?"

"Who broke Mama!?" The cry of concern came from Boy, who paused in his swordplay with a crooked stick to defend his mother from the unknown evil.

Mary ruffled his hair affectionately, "A bad man who we won't speak of anymore," she insisted, urging him back to the open lawn to continue his exercise. "We shall do all in our power to avoid his introduction and be spared the burden of an acquaintance."

Boy glowered treacherously, brandishing his stick with extra force at the invisible threat, "I'll fight him if he comes! Don't let him hurt you, either, Minney!" he beseeched, eyes wide and full of worry.

"I'm sure your father would take care of him before it came to that," their aunt remarked. "You know he would never let anyone hurt your mama, or your sisters."

The Brandon Boy nodded vigorously, absolutely confident in his father's ability to keep every member of their household safe and well.

Mary, too, let the incident pass, staying true to her word in avoiding Mr. Willoughby, and no more thinking of him than the wasps in the garden. She did not think him worthy of more curiosity than that. Whatever had transpired in the past had no affect on her, present or future. She was a Brandon, after all, and as such she would live and prosper.

Made in the USA
Columbia, SC
02 April 2024

33944128R00121